STRIKEZONE

STRIKEZONE

DAVID F. NIGHBERT

ST. MARTIN'S PRESS

NEW YORK

Design by Sharleen Smith

Library of Congress Cataloging-in-Publication Data

Nighbert, David F.
    Strikezone/David F. Nighbert.
            p.   cm.
      ISBN 0-312-02987-X
      I. Title.
    PS3564.I363S7   1989
    813'.54—dc19   89-4184
                                                                        CIP

First Edition

10 9 8 7 6 5 4 3 2 1

TO MY PARENTS

ACKNOWLEDGMENTS

I wish to thank Chief Robert C. Steen and Sergeant Jack Dawson of the Galveston Police Department for their help on matters of police procedure. Any errors or exaggerations are entirely my responsibility. Special thanks also go to Temple and Charlie Lou Paysee, Tommy Townsend, Diane Wonio and Ceri Griffith for their patient hospitality.

He knew, of course, that appearances could be deceiving; but no one had ever told him what to judge by instead of appearances.

Robert Sheckley
Mindswap

CHAPTER 1

They wore black hoods. And even I'd seen enough television to know that people who covered their faces were up to no good. I was leaning on the counter listening to Juice rattle on, my back to the door, when I heard them coming. I turned as the bigger one materialized out of the darkness on the loading dock, stepped through the door, and lumbered aside. The smaller one followed, moving like he was on casters, and glided silently up to the counter.

When his eye slits veered my way, Juice blurted, "No! Not him!"

The eyes shifted back to Juice, and the arm came up. There was a black glove on the hand, a black automatic in the glove, and a black silencer on the end.

The silencer went *foot!* and kicked Juice backward. He grabbed his chest and pulled some papers off my desk. The second *foot!* spun him around. The third caught him in the back of the head and slammed him face forward into the wall. He hugged it for a moment, arms extended, then slid to the floor behind my desk.

The Shooter turned to me, glided two steps, and looked up: dark brown eyes, enlarged pupils, lots of blue in the whites.

I was bigger by six inches and fifty pounds. His buddy had me beat by another fifty, but if I could take the gun, maybe . . .

Before I could move, I was staring down the hole at the end of the silencer.

I prayed—fast—first time in years: *Dear God! Do something! Please!*

The Shooter didn't say anything, but I was sure he was grinning beneath the mask. He loved this. Better than sex. Shooting Juice had just gotten him started. He was going to get it off with me.

I couldn't speak and tried not to breathe. All I had was the silence—this moment—and I wasn't doing anything to spoil it.

The Shooter lapped up my fear like a cat with cream, waiting with the patience of a cobra in that frozen moment before it strikes.

But he didn't strike. Just when I was sure my time was up, the silencer was retracted, and the Shooter was gliding toward the doorway. He vanished without a glance, and his partner backed out behind him. I could hear the bigger one's footsteps for a few seconds, then nothing. No sound of a car starting, no squeal of tires, just the hum of fans, the buzz of fluorescent lights, a ghostly siren wailing somewhere, and my heart pounding in my ears.

CHAPTER 2

I stood there for a while after that, staring out the door, replaying the scene over and over. When I couldn't take that anymore, I turned to the phone on the counter . . . and the sight of blood stopped me cold. It was everywhere, concentrated in a mushroom-shaped stain that nearly covered the far wall, the bright, metallic smell so thick it made me gag.

I hung on long enough to call 911, then waited on the dock.

The first patrol car was there in a couple of minutes, and EMS wasn't far behind. The paramedics confirmed that Juice was dead, then left him for the County Medical Examiner, and a patrolman took my statement. More uniforms showed up for a look, followed by a police photographer, the crime lab people, then a lean black sergeant named Willis. The smell of blood was still getting to me, and Willis took pity, suggesting we talk down at the station.

The police were headquartered behind City Hall in a modern, two-story, preform concrete, beige brick and glass structure they shared with the fire department. We entered through a back door, climbed two flights of concrete stairs and crossed an

3

empty squad room into a tiny office barely big enough for the two of us, plus a small desk and two chairs. We squeezed in behind the desk knee to knee, and he took me through the story. We were working on a second draft when he was called away.

Ten minutes passed, then fifteen, and I'd had my fill of waiting by the time a man stuck his head in the door. "Mr. Cochran?"

"That's me."

"I'm Lieutenant Parkinson." He was a gentle-faced man in his mid-forties, looking more like a teacher than a cop in his bow tie, horn-rims, and plaid jacket. "Why don't you come down to the captain's office? You'll be more comfortable."

The office was roomy, with several chairs, an executive desk, and a map of Galveston covering most of one wall.

Parkinson nodded at an attractive woman setting up a tape recorder. "Detective Flanagan will record this, if you don't mind."

"Okay with me." I just wanted to get on with it.

He gestured at a chair, then took the one behind the desk and glanced at some notes written on what looked like a pay envelope.

When Detective Flanagan finished positioning her microphones and took a seat to my right, Parkinson asked, "Why was the door open?"

"I beg your pardon?"

"You reported that the two men stepped through an open door. I was wondering why it was open on a hot night like this."

"The AC's busted."

He made a note. "Could you describe the black hoods?"

"Tailor-made, neatly stitched eyeholes."

"Made of what?"

"Black velvet . . . like they paint Elvis on."

He could have given Jack Webb deadpan lessons. "Tell me about the gunman."

"Built like Ozzie Smith."

"Who?"

"'The Wizard,' shortstop for the Cards."

"Cards?"

"Cardinals. National League franchise, Saint Louis." I resisted the impulse to ask if he knew where that was.

"And his partner?"

"Built like Laurence Taylor."

"Who?"

"Linebacker, Giants, National Football League. They're called the New York Giants even though they play in New Jersey. Make sense to you?"

"Can you tell me anything else about the two men?"

"What I could see through the eyeholes, the Shooter's skin was brown."

"Brown?"

"More *café au lait* than chocolate."

"Hispanic?"

"Could be."

"Anything distinctive about his partner, other than his size?"

"He had yellow eyes."

"Like a canary?"

"More like an old newspaper."

Parkinson liked that. "And you say the Shooter moved like he was on wheels?"

"Casters. Like a shortstop, smooth as silk."

He made a note, then examined me for a moment. "You played professional baseball, I understand—five and a half years in the minor leagues, three weeks in the Majors in the summer of 'seventy-eight, then you were demoted to the minors and retired in July of that year."

"I thought you didn't know baseball."

"I don't." He nodded at Detective Flanagan. "*She* knows baseball."

She smiled. I had been too preoccupied to take much notice of her before. Early thirties. Curly red hair. Green eyes. Freckles under her tan. Easily the prettiest cop I'd ever met.

Parkinson continued: "You and Mr. Hanzlik were in the minor leagues together?"

"That's right."

"You were friends?"

"Yeah."

"Close?"

"At one time."

"What happened?"

"Guess it wore out."

"Why?"

I shrugged. "He was a slob and a liar."

"Define slob."

"Fat and sweaty, belly out to here."

"Define liar."

"He didn't always tell the truth."

"Did he steal from you?"

Was he guessing? "Some."

"How much?"

"Hard to say. He did the books up until a month ago."

"Hundreds or thousands?"

"Hundreds. Juice was strictly small-time."

The lieutenant pulled a piece of paper out of a jacket pocket. "When did you hire Amanda Williams?"

I nodded at the paper. "Isn't it there?"

He repeated patiently, "When did you hire Ms. Williams?"

"A little over a month ago."

That appeared to jibe with his note, which he put back in his pocket. "You employed her because you caught your partner jimmying the books?"

"Uh-huh."

"How'd you find out?"

"I was having trouble on an estimate and was going through the files looking for a comparison. And I noticed that some of the figures didn't look right."

"So you confronted him with it?"

"After I was sure."

"And that's when your friendship started to deteriorate?"

"It didn't help."

"The last straw?"

"Something like that."

"Did you fight about it?"

"Fight?"

"Did the matter ever come to fisticuffs?"

"We got into a scuffle."

"Define scuffle."

"Grown men acting like children."

"Who won?"

I recalled a black eye, a busted nose, and a bloody lip. "Call it a draw."

"So, you decided to have him killed."

I stared at him for a moment. "What do you watch for? A twitch of the lip, a betraying blink of the eye, or do you rely on the incautiously blurted word?"

A smile made it as far as his eyes. "Do you mind if I ask a personal question?"

"What if I said yes?"

"Were you sleeping with Hanzlik's wife?"

"She left him. Moved back to Houston months ago."

"Before that?"

I grinned. "She was fatter than Juice."

"Some like them fat."

"Not me." I let my eyes slip to Detective Flanagan and thought for a moment she was going to wink.

"Why do you call him Juice?" Parkinson asked.

"His word for beer. Always saying 'Toss me the juice.'"

"How much did he steal from you?"

"Like I said, I can't be sure. The books were science fiction."

"People have been killed for less."

"People have been killed for no reason at all."

"But you *had* a reason."

I held up a hand. "If I'm being accused of something, Lieutenant, I want a lawyer."

"No accusation, Mr. Cochran. It's merely routine to explore the motives of those closest to the victim."

"In other words, I *am* a suspect."

"At this point, so is practically everybody on the island."

"Do you plan on giving them *all* the third degree?"

He sat back, honestly surprised. "If you feel I've been overly zealous, I apologize. I know some people find my manner offensive."

"I can't imagine why."

Detective Flanagan covered her mouth.

Parkinson glanced at her, then back at me. "May we continue? Or do you wish to call your lawyer?"

"I'll go it solo for now, but I reserve the right to change my mind."

"Of course." He consulted another scrap of paper. "Do you know the name Juan Domingo Sanchez?"

My stomach lurched. "I didn't have *him* killed, either."

"No," he agreed. "You killed him."

It was a statement of fact, not an accusation, but I couldn't help feeling defensive. "A fastball killed him. It was an accident. And I don't see what it has to do with Juice's death."

"You'd had fights with Sanchez, hadn't you?"

"Once or twice."

"In fact, you were famous enemies, weren't you?"

"I don't know about famous. We may have been headline news in the Pawtucket *Sun,* but I doubt the *New York Times* gave us much space." I was sweating and knew Parkinson had noticed.

"Isn't it true that Sanchez once gave you a beating so severe you had to sit out the last month of the season?"

I got to my feet. "As I understand it, a man can be tried for a crime only once."

"It was a coroner's inquest," he said mildly, "not a trial."

I crossed my arms and took a stand. "I'm not answering any more questions about Domingo Sanchez."

"Okay," he said agreeably. "Who do *you* think killed your partner?"

"I have no idea."

"Who would gain from his death?"

"Other than the world in general?"

He examined me a moment. "You don't mean that."

I was ashamed. "No."

"Do you have an option to buy his half of the business?"

"I think that was one of the clauses in the contract."

"But you're not *sure*?"

"I know his half reverts to Lorene, but I think I have first option if she chooses to sell."

"Would you buy it?"

"I might."

"Was Harvey into drugs?"

"Do you just ask whatever pops into your head?"

He didn't mind repeating himself. "Was he?"

"He was into anything that got him high."

"Marijuana?"

"Check."

"Cocaine?"

"Check."

"Pills?"

"Check. But his passion was Budweiser."

"Did he sell drugs?"

"An occasional bag of dope, maybe."

"Were you a customer?"

"I'd be a fool to tell you if I was."

He nodded, pushed back his chair and came to his feet. "I'm through with you . . . for now. But," he added before I could move, "that doesn't mean you can go, I'm afraid. Now, you get to go through it all over again with Detective Flanagan." He glanced at her. "Should I send in a chaperone?"

"Don't be silly," she said.

"I meant for him."

She blushed.

CHAPTER 3

When he was gone, Detective Flanagan asked me to sit down, then walked around the desk to take Parkinson's chair, glancing through her notes. "William Hayworth Cochran, known as Bull. Do you like being called Bull?"

I shrugged. "Everybody has a nickname in baseball, and bullish was my style on the mound."

She nodded. "Head down, eyes slit, shoulders slumped, and you seemed to grow as you went into your windup."

"How do you—?"

"I saw you pitch."

"You're kidding."

"On tape," she said. "But you don't care to be called Bull anymore?"

"Not much. There's something kind of sad about old guys called Pinky or Butch."

She smiled. "Well, Bill, let's take it again from the top."

The incident had lasted less than thirty seconds, but it took much longer with her picking at every detail. She wanted to know what kind of shoes the men wore. (Black running shoes, no visible labels.) Did I notice the make of the gun or the silencer? (No.) She asked me to estimate the height and weight of the two men. (The Shooter: five-ten, maybe 150. The Linebacker: taller than me and fifty pounds heavier, 260 or so, weight lifter.)

"The killing took place after midnight," she said. "Why were you at the office so late?"

"Juice called and got me out of bed. Said he needed to talk."

"About what?"

"He didn't say."

"How long after you reached the office did the two men arrive?"

"Couple of minutes. They must have followed me into the lot."

"And Mr. Hanzlik didn't say anything during that time?"

"Said plenty. He was wired, couldn't stand still, talking up a storm."

"About what?"

"Our years in the minors."

"Was he drunk?"

"He'd been drinking."

"Drugs?"

"Speed, maybe, the way he was pacing. But mostly he was scared."

"Of what?"

"He wouldn't say, just kept going on about what great times we'd had."

"And he didn't say anything that might offer a clue to what had scared him?"

I replayed the scene: Juice prowling, red-faced, dripping sweat, rattling on and on and . . . "There was something. I don't know if it'll help any, but at one point he said something about a friend turning on him and how it was the lowest thing a man could do. I thought he was talking about me at first, but he went on to say how glad he was that *I'd* never turned on him."

"Do you have any candidates in mind?"

"For what?"

"The betraying friend."

"God, I don't know. Talk to Juice five minutes, and you were his buddy for life. But real friends? Other than me, I guess Anna Mae Boatman and Gareth Llewellyn were the people closest to him on the island. But I can't picture either of them being involved in this."

"Mr. Hanzlik gambled?"

"Only when he was awake."

"Then he must have had friends in that sector."

"If you can call them that. There's a guy goes by the name of Phillie Dog Ruttenberg."

She smiled. "Yes, we know Mr. Ruttenberg."

"And there were two other gambler types Juice owed money to at one time: Rufus something—drove an old red Caddy convertible with steer horns on the front—"

"Rufus Jones."

"That's it. He and his partner—a big Indian who claims to be pure-blooded Apache—"

"Jim Two Feathers," she said.

"So you know them."

"There are warrants out for both men, but we think they left the area several weeks ago. Any other friends?"

"There was a Mexican woman Juice was seeing about the time Lorene left: Conchita Juarez." As she jotted down the name, I added, "And he also knew Julius Brauer."

"Of *the* Brauers?"

"That's the one."

She was impressed. "How'd they get to know each other? If you'll pardon my saying so, I wouldn't have thought he was Brauer's type." Julie was the island's most famous homosexual.

"Juice was more an employee than a friend," I felt required to explain. "Served as one of Julie's bodyguards on a trip to Central America back before I came down."

The connection seemed to please her. "Has he worked for him since?"

"Occasionally ran errands for him."

12

"That sounds like a strange thing for a man who owns a business to be doing."

"Juice had no pride when he needed cash."

"Didn't he work at the warehouse?"

"Not for a couple of years. He was never much help, and frankly I was more comfortable running it without him."

"What'd you gross last year?"

"We split about ninety thousand before taxes."

She said bluntly, "That doesn't sound like much."

"Getting better. The Bust hit us hard. Cut way down on the move-ins, and those on the way out couldn't afford a mover. But there's a lot of construction going on right now, so this year should be pretty good."

"How'd you get into this business?"

"It was Juice's idea, actually. Called me about it when I was living in New York."

"When was that?"

"Spring of 'eighty-one."

She jotted down the year, then stared at it. "And you retired from baseball in 'seventy-eight?"

"That's right."

"What did you do in between?"

"Spent a year working on my father's farm."

"In Illinois?"

"That's right."

"Didn't like farming?"

"Not much. I have a degree in ag science, but I majored in baseball."

"So you quit the farm?"

"My dad sold it."

"What'd you do after that?"

"I spent six months watching him die."

"I'm sorry."

"Me, too. Then I moved to New York."

"How'd you like it?"

"I liked the city fine, but I wasn't really doing anything. And I guess I was getting pretty bored when Juice called."

13

"So, you jumped at the chance to get into the moving business?"

"Is that skepticism?"

She grinned. "Sounds like a dullish career choice for an ex-professional athlete."

"Maybe I'd had all the excitement I could stand."

She wasn't convinced. "Maybe."

"Actually, I wasn't too hot on the idea at first. But Juice kept at me. He even flew up to talk about it—went on and on about the virtues of the Gulf Coast, the new financial frontier. Unfortunately, neither of us knew the Bust was just around the corner."

"How much was your investment?"

"A hundred and ten thousand."

"Did you borrow it?"

"No. My father left me over three hundred thousand."

"A wealthy man?"

"Land poor, he always said. But that's just farmer talk. He had eight hundred acres of prime bottom land, and selling it was probably what killed him."

"How'd Mr. Hanzlik come up with his share?"

"I don't know. I was a little surprised he could put that much together."

"Did you ask about it?"

"Yeah. Said he'd had some luck."

"Gambling?"

"That was my assumption."

"He was from this area, wasn't he?"

"From Texas, yeah. Born in Lubbock, raised in Houston."

She made another note. "At what time did he call you last night?"

"Eleven-fifteen or so."

"Wake you up?"

"No."

"But you were in bed?"

I nodded.

"Alone?"

"Is that relevant?"

"Could be."

"How?"

She smiled to ease the sting. "I just ask questions. The lieutenant says that's all there is to it. You keep asking till the answers start to make sense."

"Will you let me know when that happens?"

"You'll be one of the first," she promised.

"For the record, I was alone. I was reading."

"Ah."

I covered a yawn and glanced at my watch: 3:34 A.M. "Do the condemned get a last meal around here?"

"I'm sorry," she said. "Are you hungry?"

"Starving."

She snapped her notebook closed. "We're through with you . . . for now."

"That's just the way the lieutenant said it, with the same little pause before 'for now.'"

She laughed. "Guess it's catching." Switching off the recorder, she added, "We'll be keeping your home and business under surveillance for the next few days."

"Sounds good to me."

"We thought it might."

"Care to join me for an early breakfast?"

"Can't. Sorry. Have to talk to the lieutenant."

"I could stand a fifteen-minute wait."

She blessed me with a tolerant smile. "Not this morning, Bill. But thank you."

"Just for the record, do you ever date suspects?"

"The department frowns on it."

"How do *you* feel about it?"

This time, she *did* wink. "Frowns give you wrinkles."

15

CHAPTER 4

I wasn't really hungry—just hadn't wanted to be alone—so I passed on breakfast and pointed my pickup toward home, which was only a dozen or so blocks from the police station. The humidity had lifted a little, and the temperature was at its predawn coolest, in the high seventies. So I rolled down the windows and took in the sweet air, smelling pleasantly of damp grass and oleander, flavored with a salty tang of the gulf.

I pulled out of the lot and followed the trolley tracks south on Rosenberg, easing across Broadway past the Texas Heroes Monument. Broadway was the main street, swooping down out of I-45 and cutting the eastern third of the island in half west to east, a wide boulevard with a tree-lined median. As though it were contagious, Rosenberg acquired a tree-lined median of its own as it became 25th Street south of Broadway.

I turned left on Avenue M into one of Galveston's typically mixed neighborhoods: Victorian mansions alternating indiscriminately with dingy little cottages and modern duplexes. The island's architectural chaos accorded with my taste for disorder.

It was a good little town, not great, not very exciting or challenging. It wouldn't be accurate to say, for example, "If you can make it there, you'll make it anywhere." Making it in Galveston didn't signify much, but that was okay with me. What was left of my father's three hundred grand wouldn't have lasted long in a big city, but down here it could hold the wolves at bay for a long time to come.

It was a pleasant enough place to live if you weren't poor, as were too many of the 63,000 residents. Like most tourist resorts, it was basically a one-industry town, and there wasn't much opportunity for upward mobility. The result was an imbalanced economic structure, disproportionately heavy at top and bottom. There were the old Galveston families who had made their money before the turn of the century when the island was the Gulf Coast's major resort, shipping port, and financial center—"the Wall Street of the Southwest." There were the doctors, nurses, and technicians employed by the University of Texas Medical Branch. There were those who ran the fishing and what shipping was left after the Houston ship channel siphoned off the lion's share. There were the Texas City refineries and NASA up on the mainland. But the major industry was still tourism, and the employment it provided was largely seasonal and low-income.

There was no sign of the promised surveillance when I stopped under the streetlight in front of my house. There were four other cars on the block: a rusted hulk that hadn't moved for months, a station wagon and a Volkswagen bus, both familiar, and the red Ford pickup that belonged to my next-door neighbor. I would have felt a lot better with a patrol car in sight.

My home was a three-story Victorian gingerbread built in 1883, now in the process of restoration. It needed work, probably always would, but it didn't look bad at all in the glow of the streetlight.

I only wished I'd remembered to leave a light on. The walk passed between two thick-trunked oaks, perfect for an ambush, so I walked up the driveway until I was beyond them. Then I crossed to the walk and turned my attention to the porch. The first story was raised eight feet to protect against flooding, and white latticework covered the open space between floor level and the ground. Most of the porch was in shadow, but nothing moved while I watched.

Too tired to stand in the yard the rest of the night, I took a deep breath at the foot of the steps and went up them on tiptoe. I froze in a crouch at the top, glancing right and left, but saw no hooded figures. The porch creaked sharply as I started across, and I froze again at the sound. But nothing stirred.

Once inside, I went around the first floor searching for intruders, turning on all the lights, checking the latches on the windows and the locks on the doors. But nothing appeared to have been tampered with.

I saved the study, my pride and joy, for last. It was the result of months spent stripping layers of paint from the hand-carved mahogany paneling, chimneypiece, and built-in bookcases. The red leather chesterfield and armchairs and the mahogany desk had belonged to my father.

I switched on the big window-unit air conditioner and took my stash from the secret compartment in the kneehole of the desk. It was good Thai weed, not kick-ass but very mellow, and mellow was what I had in mind. Juice had sold it to me, and that seemed appropriate.

It didn't help much. May have dulled my anxiety a bit, but it also left me open to a flood of memories. Fresh ones of Juice's death that made me want to throw up and more distant ones of him at other times that left me depressed. But, if I avoided those, that only left me with memories of Domingo Sanchez, and they gave me the shakes.

I wouldn't let myself look at the night I killed him, ten years earlier. Not yet. I wasn't ready for that. But I ran through what came after: the confusion of lights and faces, cameras and microphones, press and police, lawyers and judges. And questions, the same ones, over and over. But the worst memories were of the letters and phone calls, some from white people happy to see any brown-skinned bugger bite the dust, others from blacks or Hispanics who likewise assumed that the act had been racially motivated. Several claimed to be relatives of the deceased, one from a twelve-year-old boy who said he was Domingo's brother. Several were written in Spanish, and a Latin ballplayer reluctantly translated a few of them for me. They went on at varying lengths, but the general consensus was that Domingo had died a cruel and painful death, and they hoped I would do the same.

It got so bad that I finally had my phone disconnected and stopped reading my mail. But, believe it or not, I eventually reached the point where I could go for as much as a week without remembering that I had once killed a man.

When I'd had all the remembering I could stand, I poured a glass of orange juice, turned off the lights, and headed up the stairs to my bedroom.

I was reaching for the doorknob when the floor creaked behind me. Before I could react, my face was slammed into the door. The juice glass shattered, cutting into my hand. I lashed out with the other and heard a satisfying grunt as it landed. Then a punch to the kidneys dropped me to the floor, and two men waded in with fists and feet.

When I curled into a fetal knot, they jerked me off the floor. Big men, hard muscled, breathing heavily—but no more heavily than me. One threw the door open, and they dragged me into the bedroom.

"Boys, please. That's a valuable commodity you're brutalizing." It came from a chair near the windows, a smug Ivy League voice with the delivery of a classical deejay. A narrow head was silhouetted against the light from the street: dark hair, pale face, dark clothing. Not the Shooter, I thought. But there had to be a connection.

"That's Bull Cochran," the voice went on, "former terror of the International League. He once killed a man with a fastball. Billy, I must say you're not looking very bullish at the moment."

One of his henchmen snickered.

"I should tell you," the voice continued, "I was most distressed to learn that Juice had met his untimely end. I regret disturbing you in your hour of grief, but life goes on, alas, and our late and lamented friend made business commitments he is sadly no longer able to meet. Those commitments now fall to you, as his partner, and I'm certain that once I explain the situation, you'll want to do everything in your power to expedite matters. Am I right?"

"Right."

"Excellent. You see, the unfortunate Juice was in possession of two suitcases belonging to me. He stored them for a brief period in your warehouse. But when he went to retrieve them—lo and behold!—they were not to be found. All I ask is that you return my property. Do you think you can do that for me?"

"I can try."

"Try hard."

Encouragement was provided by a fist to the solar plexus and another that bounced off the side of my head.

Through the ringing in my ears, I heard "Give him the envelope," and something was stuffed into my hip pocket. "It contains the carbon of the storage contract and five hundred dollars," he said. "You'll receive another five hundred as a bonus when my luggage is returned."

"How?"

"You'll deliver them to me on the south jetty at two-thirty tomorrow morning. All the details are in the envelope. For now," he added pleasantly, "why don't you lie down?"

I was dumped onto the bed as he headed for the door. And I was sure he wasn't the Shooter. I would have recognized that gliding step.

He paused at the door and said without turning, "You'll find your telephones temporarily out of order, and one of my associates will remain nearby to ensure you don't leave the house. Another will follow you to work in the morning and track you during the day. So absolute discretion would be advised. Don't you agree?"

"Yes."

"Don't bother to get up," he said graciously. "We'll go out the way we came in."

I waited a few minutes after the last sound, then went downstairs and found the back door standing open. Assuming they

20

had picked the lock, I checked for scratches, like they do on TV, but I didn't find any. I relocked it, vowing to have a better one installed.

Then I went upstairs and washed down a handful of Tylenol with some of Galveston's brackish water. I kept the bottled stuff in the kitchen, but I didn't feel like trekking all the way back downstairs just for a glass of water.

Afterward, I examined myself in the full-length mirror. It hurt to breathe, and I thought a rib might be cracked, but all that showed was some redness on my torso. My face had taken most of the visible damage: my nose was bent and shoved to the side, my right eye was swelling shut, and my lower lip was busted. I wasn't Quasimodo, but I'd have to put my modeling career on hold for a few days.

I climbed into bed and dozed off and on until eight, then showered and had some breakfast with my Tylenol.

CHAPTER 5

I picked up Leggy Taylor on my way into work. He lived in one of the Oleander Homes, a name that evoked images of Old Southern elegance: black or Hispanic servants in white linen bowing and scraping on those fragrant summer evenings on the veranda. In this case, it was the ironic name for one of several low-income public housing projects. I saw plenty of blacks and Hispanics, but they weren't in white linen, and the eyes that caught mine were mostly challenging.

The Oleander Homes were located between 15th and 17th Streets, four square blocks of two-story brick, clapboard, and concrete-block buildings, each containing apartments for sixteen families, with rusty swings and jungle gyms and T-pipe clothesline posts visible in the open spaces behind them. The buildings were dusty and neglected, the paint jobs peeling, the screen doors as tattered as old socks. And even the kids looked tired.

Legrange Wellington Taylor was called Leggy because he was as bowlegged as an old-time cowboy and because some people laughed at a black man called Legrange or Wellington. He was fifty-three years old and skinny as a fifty-cent chicken, with a skullcap of steel wool and skin the polished mahogany of my father's desk. He was an artist when it came to packing, especially fine china, and a box he packed could be dropped from the top of the American National Insurance Co. tower without chipping a plate. Sonny Owens called it 'voodoo packin'.'

"What happen' to your face?" he asked.

"Ran into a door."

Leggy cackled. "'Bout a dozen times, from the look of it."

He didn't take a paper, own a radio or a television, and hadn't heard about Juice's murder until I told him.

After a few blocks of silent head-shaking, he said quietly, "That's just a dirty low-down cryin' shame."

I thought that pretty much summed it up.

Traffic was bumper-to-bumper in front of the warehouse because of a procession of gawkers and three TV trucks that were blocking most of my lane. Minicams and microphones were thrust at my window as I pulled up to the gate, and a policeman made me show an ID before opening it.

We had a load coming out of storage, and Sonny Owens was backing a trailer into position as I climbed the steps to the dock. There was a wide yellow ribbon stretched across the office door bearing the words POLICE LINE DO NOT CROSS, but I crossed anyway. I didn't intend to disturb any evidence, but the day's work orders were inside, and my business would grind to a halt without them. I unlocked the door and ducked under the ribbon, wondering if Lieutenant Parkinson would believe I hadn't noticed it.

It was already an oven inside, at nine o'clock, and the stink of Juice's blood took my breath away. I stayed just long enough to grab the paperwork, then locked up and handed the orders to Tony Perelli.

Tony was my right-hand man. He drove on most of the local moves, handled the forklift, and acted as foreman. He was a handsome fellow, just turned thirty, but a fondness for pasta had added forty pounds to his compact frame since he'd come to work for me. I was probably going to lose him soon, as he

23

stood to inherit some money from his dying uncle, and I frankly didn't know what I was going to do without him.

When I asked him to hold the fort for a while, he glanced at my face and said, "They do that when they shot Juice?"

I didn't want to go into it. "Yeah."

"Hope they find the fuckers." Tony was a born-again Christian and rarely used obscenities, so I knew he was upset.

All I could say was "Me, too."

Saturday was Doctor Riggins's morning for golf, but I'd persuaded him to meet me in his office at 9:30. He wasn't happy about it and made me pay for my insistence when he straightened my nose.

"That hurts," I said.

"Does it?"

"Isn't it customary to use a local anesthetic for this procedure?"

"That's for sissies," he said and went on straightening. "There's no fracture of the nasal bone here, merely a dislocation of the lateral cartilages and the cartilage of the septum."

"Ouch!"

"Did that hurt?"

He took a few X-rays, sampled my bodily fluids, and decided I'd live. No internal bleeding and no cracked or broken ribs, he assured me. He strapped the ribs with an Ace bandage to make breathing less painful, and he warned me to go easy on the lifting. But that was wasted breath since I could barely lift my arms.

A steel-gray Mercury followed me back into the lot, and I didn't need the exempt plates to tell me it was an unmarked car. Lieutenant Parkinson climbed out with Sergeant Willis. Willis was dressed for the heat in seersucker trousers, open-necked shirt, and a straw hat, but the lieutenant was still in his jacket and bow tie. Just looking at him made me sweat.

Willis doffed his hat, and Parkinson asked, "What happened to your face?"

24

"Ran into a door."

He adjusted his horn-rims. "Can we go into the office?"

"Hot in there."

"Hot out here," he said. But after one whiff of the office, he agreed: "Maybe the warehouse *would* be better."

Willis rumbled, "Yay-uh."

I indicated the rusty stains on the wall. "Can I clean this up?"

The lieutenant nodded. "The lab people got all they needed." I could see him fitting my story to the scene, running his eyes from the door to the counter and back again.

I unlocked the door to the warehouse, wondering if I should tell him about my late-night visitors. If I did, he'd want to see the suitcases and would probably insist on opening them. And the Deejay's instructions had been explicit: the straps and metal seals must be intact when they were delivered. Or else. The "else" part was left vague, but I had no trouble imagining possibilities. On the other hand, I didn't fancy making that rendezvous alone.

I was still trying to decide what to do when Parkinson asked, "Do you mind if we wander around and ask your men some questions?"

"Do I have a choice?"

"Not really," he conceded. "But I'll try not to slow down your work any more than necessary."

The warehouse was a rectangular box running a hundred feet by two hundred. The dock was twelve feet deep and stretched the full two hundred feet across the front, with two big roll-up power doors at the loading bays. The first twenty feet at the south end of the dock had been walled in to serve as an office, with one door opening onto the dock and the other set at a right angle to the first, leading into the warehouse.

I propped open both doors and set up a fan to blow the smell toward the parking lot. Then I strolled out onto the dock, where the boys were loading the trailer.

Sonny Owens sidled over and drawled, "I was real sorry to hear about Juice. Hard way to go."

"Know an easy one?"

He hooked his thumbs in his jeans and said, "Reckon some're easier than others."

He had me there.

Sonny had the classic redneck look down to the ducktailed flattop, Camels rolled up in the sleeve of his T-shirt, and a Marine Corps tattoo on his right biceps. But, in spite of appearances, he was basically a gentle soul who found more than adequate stimulation in driving his rebuilt Peterbilt and sharing a waterbed with his wife, Charlie Lou.

Sonny was one of a number of independent truckers who worked out of Galveston. They weren't employees; more like short-term partners, peers of the road. Since he was taking a load to San Antonio this afternoon, I asked him to speak to Parkinson first.

Tony had some deliveries to make, so I suggested he follow Sonny.

When Leggy heard the news, he camped, "Always enjoy a word with the *po*-lice."

But Randy Oliver's excitement seemed genuine. Randy was Sonny's nineteen-year-old cousin, a lean six-three, on a basketball scholarship at the University of Texas. He actually seemed to enjoy the work here, which required a well-developed streak of masochism in midsummer.

Mariano Santiago just nodded. He wasn't a talker, but that was okay with me. It was nice to have somebody around who never complained. Mariano was my age, with the lithe strength and impassive face of an Apache warrior, black hair to his shoulders, black eyes regarding the world with intelligent detachment.

I was in no condition for manual labor, so I took over Tony's job, checking off items as they were loaded into the trailer.

Randy reported to me after talking with Parkinson. "They asked me a lot of questions about Mr. Hanzlik," he said. "But I didn't know anything."

"Did you tell them that?"

26

"Uh-huh."

"Then you did fine."

I expected him to go back to work, but he didn't. He hung around, squeaking the toe of one running shoe on the concrete. I was about to ask him to stop it when he added shyly, "My grandma died last year, so I kinda know how you feel."

"How?"

"How do I *know*?"

"How do I feel?"

He thought I was making fun of him.

"I'm serious," I said. "I'm having a little trouble with feelings right now."

He nodded as though he understood. And maybe he did. Then he screwed up his face. "Kinda numb like, you know . . . kinda like it never really happened. Like maybe you dreamed it up . . . and, if you really wanted to, you could still call her up on the phone. You know?"

"Yeah," I admitted. "That's pretty close." I'd seen it happen, but Juice's death still wasn't quite real to me.

Randy was so pleased at getting it right he worked like a demon for the next half-hour.

The trailer was loaded by one o'clock, and Sonny left for San Antonio.

While the others broke for lunch, I filled a mop bucket, dumped in some ammonia, and shoved it into the office. It was one job I didn't feel I could ask anybody else to handle.

The office was still stiflingly hot, but the smell was at least tolerable. The air conditioner only blew hot air, but I turned it on to move the air around. I also switched on the desk fan, set up one of the floor fans to blow in my direction, and stripped off my T-shirt. After taking a sponge to the wall, I changed the water and took a putty knife to the tarry mass on the floor. While mopping up the stains, I noticed blood spots elsewhere and ended up doing the whole floor. After a half-dozen changes

27

of water, I sponged off the file cabinets, then moved all the stuff from the desk to the counter, so I could wash off the top.

Parkinson came in to watch me sweat and picked up one of the items I'd moved to the counter. "What's this?"

"A baseball, regulation-size, molded in brass-plated iron."

"Never seen one like it."

"Juice gave it to me."

He read the inscription aloud: "To Bull, Give 'em hell in the Bigs! Juice."

"A poet he wasn't."

"What was the occasion?"

"I was embarking on my stab at the Majors."

"He must've liked you."

"Must have."

He stared at me for a moment, then tossed me the ball and strolled out to the dock.

I felt its weight, measuring the distance to the back of his head. Just a thought.

CHAPTER 6

Parkinson intercepted me again at the utility sink as I was rinsing out the mop bucket for the last time. "Didn't get much sleep last night, did you?"

"None to speak of."

I expected him to comment on the condition of my face, but instead he asked, "Do you know many of Hanzlik's friends?"

"He didn't have friends, just good buddies." That wasn't true, but the lieutenant brought out my crusty side.

"Do you know them?"

"I gave all the names I knew to Detective Flanagan."

"Would you mind giving me a list, too?" He took them down on the back of another envelope, then asked, "Before last night, when did you see him last?"

"Wednesday afternoon. He spent some time in the office."

"Doing what?"

"I caught him going through the files."

"And?"

"I chased him out."

"Why?"

"I was still pissed at him."

"Did he seem nervous?"

"More disappointed."

"In what?"

"In me. That was Juice's way. Whenever I'd come down on him for something, he'd give me his you-don't-treat-me-right stare."

"What'd he say?"

"Asked if I'd rearranged the box file."

"What's that?"

"Okay, let's see. We handle storage as well as moving, long- and short-term contracts. And most of the long-term storage stuff goes into boxes like this." I let him examine one of the big walk-in boxes we had unloaded: constructed of gray-painted plywood, six feet high, six feet wide, ten feet deep, with a padlocked door on the front. Then I led him to the office end of the warehouse and showed him the four rows of boxes stacked three high. There were two single rows on the ends facing inward and two more standing back-to-back between them, with two aisles wide enough to accommodate the forklift. "The stacks take up about a third of the floor space, with the rest devoted to short-term storage: boxed or crated commercial shipments, furniture, and other items too big to fit in the boxes. And each storage contract is filed and tagged with a number designating an area of the floor or one of the boxes."

"*Had* you rearranged the box file?"

"Yeah. I was redistributing the loads."

"Why?"

"It was something I'd been planning to do for some time."

"You weren't trying to cut Hanzlik out of the business?"

"No. But he may have thought I was."

"Did he say what he was looking for?"

"He mentioned a partial load contract he couldn't find."

"What's a partial load?"

"One that's too small to fill a box. We store them in common boxes with other partials."

"Why couldn't Hanzlik find the contract?"

"I had the partial load contracts with me, retagging them as I rearranged the boxes."

"Did you tell him that?"

"I wasn't volunteering information."

"Did he say anything else?"

"That he thought I was his friend."

"And what did *you* say?"

I closed the door on the storage box. "I told him to get the fuck outta here."

"How do you feel about that?"

"You a cop or a shrink?"

"I'm just trying to understand you."

"Why? It's Juice you have to understand."

"He's easy. You're the mystery."

"I had nothing to do with his murder."

"Then why are you acting so guilty?"

"Because I *feel* guilty."

"But you said you didn't *do* anything."

"I didn't."

"Did you buy cocaine from him?"

"I can't afford it."

"Only marijuana?"

"Mary who?"

He didn't miss a beat. "You knew he sold such items, didn't you?"

"I'd heard."

"From whom?"

"I'd rather not say."

He nodded. "According to the coroner, his body was covered with bruises, two sets. One set was beginning to discolor, but the other was fresh, no more than twelve hours old. You don't happen to know who could have given him the beatings?"

"The bad guys, I assume."

He examined me over the top of his glasses. "The same ones who did that to your face?"

Tell him! Get him to cover you on the jetty tonight! What if

31

he doesn't cover me well enough? *Then you're dead. With the cops there, you at least have a chance. Tell him!*

I told him.

When I finished, he asked to see the instructions. "Also the envelope and the cash. We might be able to trace the bills."

He handled the instructions at the corners, then slipped it and the envelope into a plastic evidence bag. "South jetty. Good place."

"For whom?"

"Us, I hope. You think they killed Hanzlik?"

"The Deejay wasn't the Shooter, and I don't think either of the other two men who jumped me in the house was the Shooter's partner. They were big but not *that* big."

"But you assume this 'Deejay' had Hanzlik killed?"

"He didn't say."

"I'm asking what you think."

"And I'm saying I don't *know*."

He rocked back on his heels. "I don't know either."

"Can you protect me?"

"We can try."

"I'd like something stronger than that. Were your people watching my house last night?"

He nodded. "One in front, one in back."

"They didn't do a very good job."

"No."

"How'd the Deejay and his boys get past them?"

"They could have been in the house before we put it under surveillance."

"Then how'd they get out?"

"That's the question," he conceded. "We'll look into it, but it'll probably turn out that they went out across your neighbors' back yards. Either that, or one of my people was looking in the wrong direction at the wrong time."

"I didn't see anybody in front, and I looked."

"He hid his car behind the house across the street and camped out in the front parlor."

"Ah."

"We'll try to do better this time."

"I'd appreciate it."

"I'll put a man in your house."

"Only *one*?"

"And cars front and back."

"Ask them to stay awake this time."

"I'll pass along your recommendation," he said dryly.

"What about the rendezvous?"

"We'll have an army. The boys love this cowboy stuff."

"I'm a little . . . nervous about this."

"That's understandable," he said. "Do you have a gun permit?"

"No."

"Ever carried a piece?"

"Not yet."

"Too late to learn by tonight," he said. "Let's find those suitcases."

I'd filed the several dozen partial load contracts in a manila envelope on a shelf under the counter, where Juice had had no reason to look. It didn't escape me that he might still be alive if I'd told him about the envelope, but I tried not to dwell on the thought.

The original contract listed the stored items as two gray Samsonite suitcases, and the new box number was in the upper right-hand corner: D-4a. "D" gave me the row; "4" gave me the stack; and "a" told me it was floor level. For ease of access, all partial loads were stored at floor level.

Finding the box was easy. I led them straight to it. Unfortunately, the suitcases weren't inside.

"Now what?" Parkinson asked.

"Maybe we should try *B*-four-a."

"Why?"

"Sounds like D-four-a."

But they weren't in B-4a, C-4a, or A-4a, which was as far as it went, as there were only four rows of storage boxes.

"How many boxes all together?" Parkinson asked.

"A hundred and twenty." I checked the chart. "Eighty-six in use."

He took me into the office, which now stank of ammonia. "Think you can handle it with the help you have."

"You want me to look through *all* the boxes?"

"Has to be done."

"My people are on overtime now."

"You say you're being watched, and I don't want to spook them by bringing in any more cops."

"I guess that makes sense."

"Good. I have to leave now, but Willis will stay to help."

Amanda Williams, the bookkeeper, phoned during the search to say she'd come home to find a message from the police on her answering device. "They want to see your books," she crisply concluded.

"Then you'll have to hand them over."

"*Both* sets?"

"It's probably Juice's creative version they want to see."

Dropping her usual cool formality, she said sincerely, "I was sorry to hear about his death, Mr. Cochran. I know how it feels to lose a friend. So if there's anything I can do, you just let me know. You hear?"

"I hear," I said. "And thanks."

We searched the eighty-six filled boxes, finding a number of suitcases, none of which fit the description or were tagged Harvey Hanzlik. Then we opened the remaining thirty-four boxes that were reputedly empty. They were.

Detective Willis reported the news to Parkinson, then handed me the receiver.

"Is there any place you haven't looked?" the lieutenant asked.

"None I can think of."

"Have you searched the rest of the warehouse?"

"No, but—"

"You'll have to do that, you know."

34

"I thought you people did the searching."

"I've explained why I don't want to bring any more cops into this right now. We need those suitcases, and we didn't find them at Hanzlik's house. I'll try to locate some that match the description, but it would help if we knew what they contained."

"So we're going through with this?"

"If you're still game."

"Maybe after I've had a nap."

"Maybe isn't good enough," he said sharply. "I'm not setting this up and having you pull out at the last minute. The chief frowns on wasting taxpayers' money."

"I'll *be* there. Just keep the bad guys out of my house."

"I have three people in position, one who'll go inside with you. Feel better?"

"Some. But isn't the Deejay likely to notice all this activity?"

"Which do you want," he asked, "protection or discretion?"

"Protection."

"Thought so. See you on the jetty."

CHAPTER 7

I left home just before two A.M., sharing the cab of my pickup with the two gray suitcases the police had supplied, took Avenue M down to Seawall Boulevard, and headed east. Commercial development cut off at First Street, where the Boulevard started across the East End flats. It shot straight out to the Galveston Bay channel, with the Bolivar lighthouse visible at the end, blinking on the opposite shore. The boulevard was elevated over the flats, forming the windward edge of the seawall, which rose in an asphalt incline to the left. East Beach veered away to the right, across the lagoon and another expanse of boggy grassland, where the shell of an unfinished apartment complex stood with empty eyes and two spotlighted condominium towers rose like futuristic tombstones.

Just before the end of the boulevard, I cut right onto Boddeker Drive. It crossed over the inlet to the lagoon and dipped down through the wetlands toward the jetty. To the left, with their backs to Big Reef, sat a seafood restaurant, a bait shack, a filling station, and a small diner touting BEER WINE & BUR-

GERS. Beyond that the wetlands gave way to sand flats as the road neared the southeasternmost limit of Galveston Island.

I'd always loved the windswept rawness of the south jetty, the rolling sand and frothy reefs, the encroaching tide pools and shifting dunes. But the city had almost ruined it for me a few years earlier by converting it into a municipal beach. It was called Apffel Park now, in honor of a former mayor, complete with admission booths, concrete picnic tables, and a concessions building that did a booming business in video games.

Everything was closed and dark at this time of the morning, but the area was getting good use as a lovers' lane. I turned east, as the pavement ran out beyond the empty admission booth, and followed tire tracks past a parking lot of campers, pickups, and vans, with charcoal grills, blankets, and air mattresses scattered on the sand. The cars ran out after about fifty yards, but the smell of hickory smoke and coconut oil lingered.

I'd spotted no police cars, but any of the vehicles I had passed could have contained policemen. Parkinson had assured me that my cover would be in place.

My instructions were to head east for a tenth of a mile, then pull over to the dunes and stop. I was supposed to be in position at 2:30 but arrived about ten minutes early.

It was an overcast night, the air heavy and unusually still. The mosquitoes were out in force, but I felt too closed in with the windows up, so I kept them rolled down and dared the mosquitoes to do their worst.

The jetty was well off to my right, a narrow stone breakwater reaching into the mouth of the Inner Bar channel, protecting the entrance to Galveston Harbor and the Houston ship channel. A line of freighters awaiting admission arced around to the southwest, adding their lights to those of the oil and natural gas platforms. The revolving beacon of the lighthouse on the tip of the jetty gave me periodic glimpses of the *Velma I,* a hundred yards straight ahead. She lay tipped on her side, a shrimper that had washed up on Big Reef in a late winter storm.

2:30 came and went.

I was panting like I'd run a mile, but couldn't catch a breath. The air was all heat and moisture, no oxygen.

2:40.

I couldn't produce enough saliva to swallow because all the liquid in my body was leaking out through the skin. My shirt was drenched, and my crotch felt like I'd peed on myself.

2:50.

I kept jerking my head around, trying to do a 360 like that girl in *The Exorcist*.

2:55. Nothing. Then 3:00.

I was expecting the guys in the black hoods, expecting to see them appear over the dunes to my left, the smaller one gliding ahead, arm lifting—flash, kick, death. That's what I was expecting. But it wasn't what I got.

I heard a rhythmic squeaking sound and caught a flicker of movement through the rear window. I threw open the door and rolled out of the pickup.

I was still rolling when the squeaking became a sustained squeal. Then sand was kicked in my face, and a voice said, "Señor Co-co-ran?"

It was a boy sitting on a bicycle.

I glanced around as I climbed to my feet, but there were no hooded figures in sight. Just me and the boy.

"Señor Co-co-ran?"

"Cochran. That's me."

He handed me an envelope, then turned his bike and pedaled away.

I tore the envelope open as I headed for the light from the pickup. It contained a folded sheet of paper with five words lettered in block capitals with black crayon:

YOU TOLD
SHAME ON YOU

I heard a noise behind me and turned as two dark figures appeared over the dunes. I dove into the truck and made a grab for the key, but I was shaking so badly I pulled it out of the

38

ignition. The ring dropped to the floor, and I banged my head on the steering wheel as I bent to pick it up.

I was still groping for the ring when I heard "Don't let the boy get away" and recognized Parkinson's voice.

He walked over. "You okay?"

I lowered my head to the steering wheel and groaned.

"You moved pretty fast," he said.

"Directly into the path of a vehicle."

"Lucky it was a Schwinn instead of a Camaro. Can I see the note?"

He read it and slipped it into a plastic evidence bag. Then he pulled out his walkie-talkie. "Party's over, boys. You can come on in now."

An engine roared, and a three-wheeler exploded into view, as half a dozen cops scrambled over the dunes, many carrying high-powered rifles with nightscopes.

"Couldn't you find any more help?"

"You asked for cover, right?"

"I didn't expect all this."

"Did you spot them?"

"No, but maybe somebody else did."

He shrugged, conceding the point, then informed his assault force that there would be no shoot-'em-up tonight.

The announcement evoked some grumbling and a few good-natured insults, but they'd had their playtime.

As they dispersed, Willis came back with the boy and the bike. "His name's Miguel, and he don't habla Ingles. A big gringo spoke to him in Spanish and slipped him a twenty to pedal out here and hand Señor Co-co-ran the envelope."

Parkinson gave the boy a stick of gum and squatted beside him. After a brief conversation in Spanish, the lieutenant reported that the gringo had worn a dark suit and had mirrors on his eyes.

He turned to Willis. "Probably won't do any good, but we'll take him down to look at some pictures. Why don't you try to find out where he lives, and we'll get his momma to go with us." As his car pulled up, he told me, "We'll follow you home."

* * *

Officer Chin met me at the door and walked around the house with me, all three stories, checking windows and doors. After he went back downstairs, I smoked a joint hanging out of the bedroom window. If they wanted to arrest me for it, let them. I'd had a hard day.

The joint made me hungry, so I went down and made a couple of sandwiches, one for Chin. I ate mine watching him lay out a hand of solitaire. He asked if I wanted to play some gin rummy, but I didn't feel like it. I hadn't really slept in over thirty-six hours, but I didn't feel like going to bed either. Fatigue poisons were making me hyper, and I felt like *doing* something: going for a run or a swim, climbing a mountain. Instead, I went into the back parlor and shot some pool.

The back parlor contained my weights, exercise bike, rowing machine, and the pool table. I'd found it in a storage room in the old Belmont Hotel. The table had had no felt or legs at the time, and the owners had told me I could have it if I could move it, which was no mean feat, given the weight of the six-inch slate bed. Since then, I had invested a couple of hundred dollars on felt and legs, and I had been offered two thousand for it a week earlier.

I polished off a few racks, then took my stash and a glass of orange juice up to my room.

CHAPTER 8

The warehouse was closed on Sunday, so I slept until one. I awoke stiff and sore. My right eye was swollen into a squint; both eyes were purpling nicely, and the lump on my lip gave me a constant sneer. I couldn't think of anything to do for the lip, but I took a cover-up stick to both eyes. It didn't help much.

Parkinson and Willis came by at 2:30 and drove me to the funeral home to pay my respects to Juice's remains. We weren't allowed to see those remains, of course, since the Shooter's third slug had removed a chunk of his face on its way out. So the guest of honor was represented by a flower-bedecked walnut casket.

I was surprised at the turnout—maybe forty or fifty people—and the floral tributes took up most of one wall. Their combined odor was sweet enough to give you pimples, but Juice would have been tickled pink.

The chapel was really just a carpeted room, with a few couches and folding chairs scattered around the perimeter. The people were grouped in clumps, like at a cocktail party. The

41

conversation was a bit more subdued, of course, and the laughter suitably restrained. And there were tears. You didn't get much of that at cocktail parties, at least not this early in the afternoon.

Many of the Houston relatives were holding handkerchiefs or wads of damp tissue. Juice's brother Bobbie, who'd flown down from Amarillo, kept breaking into sobs every time he tried to speak. As far as I knew, Bobbie hadn't seen his brother in ten years, and I wondered uncharitably if Juice had owed him money.

Then there was the mother, Barbara Sue Hanzlik, whose wails could be heard on entering. She was in high dirge mode, making as much racket as a mob of professional mourners: keening wails alternating with shrill cries of "Oh, my bay-beee! Oh, my Harvey! They killed my bay-beee bo-eee!" and similar demonstrations of motherly concern she'd never exhibited while Juice was alive. Strangers were moved; those who knew her were embarrassed.

Anna Mae Boatman, the closest thing to a real mother Juice had ever known, came over to give me a hug. She was so thin and frail-looking that I was afraid to squeeze too hard, but there was surprising strength in her skinny arms. She was in her eighties, all bone and mummified flesh, face wrinkled like a sun-dried grape, blue eyes bright and clear.

"Listen to that fool woman," she whispered. "She's been going on like that for half an hour now, and I'm only hangin' around to see how long she can keep it up. I bet Hiram Satterfield ten dollars she was good for at least another hour. What do you think?"

"I'd say your money was safe."

She tilted her head up to examine me and said, "That's some face you got."

"Bad?"

"'Nough to scare children."

"And grannies?"

She gave me a flinty-eyed stare. "Grannies don't scare so easy."

I laughed.

42

"So what's *your* excuse?" she asked.

"For what?"

"Not comin' to see me anymore."

"Just dumb, I guess."

"Always suspected it."

I grinned. "You see much of Juice lately?"

"Nah, he was almost as bad as you. Saw him on Thursday for the first time in . . . Lord, it must've been over a month."

"Thursday?"

"Yeah. The day before . . ." She trailed off, eyes drifting to the casket. After a moment, she sighed and asked, "Why would anybody want to kill Harvey?"

"He had some suitcases that didn't belong to him."

"He was killed over *suitcases*?"

"Over what they contained."

"Drugs?"

"Maybe."

"I tried to warn him off that cocaine," she said. "Told him I didn't see nothin' sinful in a little dirt weed. Used to smoke the stuff myself down here in the twenties, back when it grew wild in the ditches. But folks are gettin' shot over that cocaine."

She shook her head, losing her sparkle. "I knew Harvey was in trouble when he couldn't make it playin' ball. It was all he ever wanted, and not gettin' it sapped what little gumption God gave him." Tears were running down her face now. "Why didn't you take better care of him, Bull?"

I had no answer to that one.

"You know he needed somebody lookin' after him."

"I know, Granny. I'm sorry."

She blew her nose on an embroidered handkerchief, then took my arm and patted my hand. "That's all right, son. I don't mean to lay it on you. Harvey was a grown man, and he made his bed. It's just that"—her grip tightened—"his dyin' like this makes me so mad I wanta *spit*!"

"I know, Granny." I gave her a squeeze.

Barbara Sue wailed, "Harvey's gah-awn! Oh, my bay-beee's gah-awn!"

"Listen to her," Anna Mae said. "'Gone!' she says. Why, she said good riddance to that boy twenty years ago!"

"They took my bay-beee away-eee!"

"*Took* him?" Anna Mae asked. "Hell's bells, Harvey picked up his heels and *ran* the first chance he got. Lived with me six years, two blocks away from that hussy! And she never so much as called to ask about him! Does that sound like motherly love to you?"

Others were tuning in on Anna Mae's critical commentary, but I just smiled at them and agreed: "Not much."

She gave me a mischievous grin. "You paid her your respects yet?"

"Nope."

"Goin' to?"

"Think I should?"

"It's expected."

"You wanna come with me?"

"Oh, no. When we get close, sparks fly. I'll just trail along an' watch."

Barbara Sue Hanzlik was a big, bosomy woman, still handsome in her fifties. She was garbed in black, of course—ruby lips visible through her black veil—and was surrounded by a bastion of comforters. One sat on either side anchoring her to the couch, while her latest paramour—a dead ringer for Ernest Borgnine—stood sentry to the rear.

When she spotted me, she threw out her arms, fetching the woman on her right a sharp clip on the chin. "Boo-ull!" she cried. "Oh, Boo-ull! They killed our bay-beee!"

Mr. Borgnine didn't like the sound of that.

When Barbara Sue started shoving her comforters off the couch to make room for me, I protested. "I really can't stay, Ms. Hanzlik. I just wanted to tell you how sorry I was—"

But she was up and on me before I could finish. Before I could break her hold, she had me on the couch in a virtual headlock, making so much noise I could no longer hear what I was trying to say.

Much embarrassment followed, with Barbara Sue clasping

44

me to her breast and ranting on about our mutual loss, while I strained gasps of air through her fog of Shalimar.

By the time I fought my way to freedom, Anna Mae was in stitches. Dabbing at her eyes, she said, "Got the grip of a stevedore, ain't she?"

I heard "Bull!" and looked around to see Gareth Llewellyn parting the crowd, his wife, Sybil, trailing calmly in his wake. Gareth was my height but a good deal heavier, with a rosy moon-shaped face, a balding dome, and a fringe of graying hair. He was a respected kidney specialist who was paid exorbitant fees for consultations, but he looked like he belonged in a pub or leaning over a paddock fence.

He crushed my hand and granted me a peck at Sybil's cheek.

She caressed my swollen face. "You should put ice on that."

"Wanna come home and nurse it for me?"

"None of that now," Gareth objected. "At least wait till I turn my back."

Syb crossed her arms. "We're waiting."

Gareth laughed.

She was much prettier than her husband but matched him in generosity of spirit. They were the kind of couple that gave wealth a good name and brightened any gathering they entered.

When I tried to introduce Anna Mae, Sybil informed me, "We're old golf buddies. She spends even more time at the club than I do."

Gareth said, "I played her nine last week and made the mistake of spotting her five strokes."

Anna Mae punched his arm. "Let it be a lesson."

"Right," he said sourly. "Never gamble with anyone over seventy."

As Sybil pulled Anna Mae aside for a chat, I said, "I thought you two were down in the islands."

"Got back on Tuesday." He jutted his chin toward the casket. "I understand you were there when it happened."

"Yeah."

"Can't imagine."

"Don't even try."

He examined my face. "The killers do that?"

"Another pair."

"Connected?"

"The police think so."

"Are they protecting you?"

"So far."

"If there's anything you need," he said, "you've only to ask."

"I'm all right now. But thanks."

"The offer stands." His eyes drifted back to the coffin. "Saw Juice before we left. Seemed excited. Said he had something hot in the offing."

"May have been what killed him."

He nodded, fondling his lower lip, unable to take his eyes off the walnut box.

Sybil gave him a nudge. "Did you ask him?"

He growled, "Patience, woman," and told me, "We were hoping to find you here. Syb and I wanted to invite you to the house on Wednesday. It's to be a bit of an unofficial wake, *sans* corpus, for his closest friends."

Sybil said, "I invited Anna Mae, but it seems she already has an engagement."

"What's this?" he asked.

"Any other evening would be fine," Anna Mae insisted, "but Wednesday's poker night."

Gareth arched a brow. "I'd have pegged you as more of the bridge club type."

She made a face. "Bridge is for sissies and old people. The money's in poker. And Wednesday night takes care of my greens fee for the week."

Gareth laughed. "Now I see how you can afford all those trips to Mazatlán."

"No," she said, "it's my putter that gets me to Mazatlán."

He chuckled and told me, "Since we can't deprive Madame Boatman of her livelihood, it appears it'll just be the three of us. Will you come?"

"Love to."

"Good." He clapped me on the back. "We'll see that Juice is mourned in the proper fashion."

46

CHAPTER 9

On the way out to the car, Parkinson asked, "How do you know Doctor Llewellyn?"

"Juice introduced us years ago, just after I came down."

"You seemed friendly."

"He and Syb are good company. I go out to their place to eat barbecue and ride their horses. I've also been out in their boat and up in their plane."

Willis drove, and Parkinson quizzed me over the back of the seat. "How did he and Hanzlik meet?"

"Don't know. May have been through the Strand Street Theater. Gareth is on the board of directors, and Juice was in a couple of plays there."

"He was an actor?"

"Yeah. Surprised me, too. Saw him do the sheriff in *Bus Stop*."

"How was he?"

"A lot better than I expected."

"How well do you know Mrs. Boatman?"

I shrugged. "Met her about fifteen years ago. She used to fly up to see Juice play ball several times a season. And I saw quite a bit of her right after I moved down here."

"Where does she get her money?"

I grinned. "To hear her tell it, from poker and golf."

"How's that?"

"She's a hustler."

"Must be good at it. She does a lot of traveling."

"I know she gets social security and a railroad pension—her husband was an engineer for thirty years—plus some investments, I think—she's mentioned stocks a few times. And she sold the house in Houston for a bundle back during the housing boom."

"What was her relationship with Hanzlik?"

"Her name was on the list I gave you. Didn't you talk to her?"

"Detective Flanagan took her statement. But I'd like to hear what *you* think."

"A great old lady. No blood relation of Juice's, but she's the only one who ever cared anything about him. Saw him through high school and into baseball."

"And you took over from there?"

"What do you mean by that?"

"Just that he always seemed to need a keeper."

"A *friend*. Everybody needs friends. Juice just relied on his more than most."

I set up the hibachi on the front porch and started the charcoal. I usually did my grilling on the back patio, but Officer Chin had asked me to stay where he could see me.

I was putting the steaks on when Detective Flanagan showed up with a bottle of wine and a steak of her own.

"How'd you *know*?" I asked.

"I radioed ahead."

Chin nodded and grinned.

48

The detective took a look at my face and asked, "Does that hurt?"

"Not as much as my ribs," I'd often found sympathy to be an effective romantic ploy.

We ate in the dining room under the ceiling fan, discussing the virtues of central air conditioning. I quoted them the installation estimates and explained that I had been reluctant to sink so much into a white elephant I might never be able to sell. Both pretended to understand, but I caught a shared look that said they considered my attitude a bit miserly.

After dinner, Chin went back to his place in the front parlor, leaving me alone with Detective Flanagan, whom I was now allowed to call Molly.

We talked about many things. I asked how she'd ended up in police work, and she said it was a long story. So I asked for the short version.

"My uncle was a cop in Dallas. He was killed trying to save a hostage in a kidnapping, and I suppose I grew up with the idea that cops help people."

"Still feel that way?"

She shrugged. "The hardest part was getting used to the idea that some people don't *want* my help."

"How's the case going?"

"Tedious."

"What've you been doing?"

"Well, yesterday I viewed Harvey's autopsy."

I pictured Juice lying on stainless steel, organs on display.

"Sorry," she said.

"My fault. I asked." I took a sip of wine. "Do you get used to the blood?"

"Some do, some don't."

"You?"

"I'm still working on it."

"How long you been a cop?"

"Nine years. Went straight from Rice to the Houston Police Academy."

"How'd you end up down here?"

"I worked a joint investigation with Galveston P.D. and was impressed with Lieutenant Parkinson. He told me to holler if I ever needed a job."

"And you hollered?"

She nodded. "I filed a sexual harassment suit against my captain in Houston. Won it, too. But"—she shrugged—"I didn't feel like staying after that. When I came down here, I took a big cut in pay and had to start out as a patrol officer again, but the lieutenant helped me make it back to detective."

Inevitably, the talk drifted around to baseball. She wanted to know what it was like playing in the minors.

"I grew to hate buses but developed a real fondness for cheap hotels."

She grinned. "Must've been tough hanging on for so long."

"There are Hall-of-Famers who spent more time in the minors than I did, so there was always hope. At first I thought it was only a matter of time. As soon as I started getting my curve over for strikes, I expected things to start moving for me."

"But that didn't happen?"

"Nope. I worked on a slider, forkball, screwball, and palmball, but I couldn't find the strike zone with any of them."

She nodded. "Hard thrower, shaky control. Lifetime ERA of three-point-three-two, which isn't bad, considering all the walks. You led your minor league association in walks your first two years and finished in the top ten all six."

I shook my head in admiration. "Did you make a special study of me, or are you just a stat freak?"

"When I learned there was an ex-pitcher running a local moving company, I did some digging. I even saw a tape of your first big-league start."

I nearly choked on my wine. "I'm surprised you were willing to eat with me."

"It wasn't *that* bad."

"Don't tell *me*. I was *there*."

"You had a no-hitter going into the third."

"Unfortunately, I was also six runs down."

She stifled a laugh. "Four runs in the first really wasn't bad considering the four walks and two wild pitches. And you did strike out the side.''

"But then came the *second* inning.''

She nodded. "Two more walks, another wild pitch. Then you strike out two, and it looks like you're going to get out of it.''

"But, like in a horror movie, just when you think you're safe, the monster appears.''

"Yeah,'' she said grimly. "In the shape of a three hundred pound ump named 'Cowboy' Eddie Kendon.''

I made a growling sound. "Used to send him hate notes at Christmas.''

"*Consecutive* balk calls,'' she said in wide-eyed wonder. "I couldn't believe it. How could he *do* that?''

"Easy.''

"Two pitches, two balks, two runs scored.''

"Amazing,'' I agreed, wondering how much longer we were going to discuss it.

"Then you get out of the inning on a strikeout.''

"And, as you said, I still had my no-hitter going.''

She hid her face in her wineglass. "When you walked the lead-off batter in the third, I thought for sure they'd lift you.''

"I was praying for it.''

"Then you get the next batter to ground into a sure double play, but both are safe on an error, and you're in trouble again.''

I shrugged. "The infield had seen me clowning on the mound all afternoon and wanted their chance.''

"After two quick strikeouts, it looks like you're going to get out of it after all. But then you intentionally walk the league's leading hitter to get to the league's weakest.''

"Yeah, Bobo Rodriguez of the one forty-three batting average and one home run in five hundred and thirty-six at bats.''

"And he sends a moonshot into the second balcony. Grand Salami. Four runs scored.''

I smothered a groan. "And that was it. Too bad, really. Two more wild pitches, and I'd have tied the record.''

She grinned, then tried to look sympathetic. "I thought they

51

were squeezing the plate on you, especially in the first. And I didn't see any movement on either of the balk calls.''

"Cowboy Ed said I didn't come to a full stop in the stretch.''

"Half the pitchers in the league don't stop in the stretch—or didn't until they went balk-crazy this summer.''

"That's the game,'' I said.

"Still bitter?''

"Only when I think about it.''

CHAPTER 10

Juice's funeral was on Monday at the First Baptist Church, a red-brick colonial edifice on Tremont. As a pallbearer, I had to attend, but I didn't feel required to listen. I stood up and sat down when the others did, held a hymnal and pretended to sing when it was called for. Then I helped carry the casket out to the hearse and rode with the other pallbearers in the procession.

A black mass of clouds charged in from the west as we pulled into the cemetery, but the sun hung on gamely until we got the casket under the shelter. Then wind kicked up as the light dimmed, tearing at the canvas and sending the women grabbing for their hats. The rain came as Juice was lowered into the ground, marching on us in rippling shrouds, lashing in at a steep angle, blowing under the shelter and riffling the canvas. The preacher wrapped up the service quickly with a brief prayer, but people were sprinting for their cars before he could get out the Amen.

Juice's wife, Lorene, had fainted at the church, but Barbara Sue saved her swoon for the big finish. As the casket started its descent, she poured out of her chair, and was carried to her hired limo by a phalanx of middle-aged hearties. Anna Mae countered these histrionics with quiet, sorrowful dignity. Of the four women in Juice's life, only the girlfriend, Conchita Juarez, was absent, no doubt realizing that she wouldn't be welcomed by the others.

Gareth and Sybil tried to talk Anna Mae into letting them take her home, but she wanted to stay, and I promised I'd look after her. We sat for another ten minutes, collecting a gloss of wind-blown rain. Then I wrestled the squall for possession of my umbrella as I walked her out to her fire engine red motor scooter.

"Why don't you let us run you home in the patrol car?" I said. "You'll drown on that thing."

"No, sir," she insisted. "You just hold that umbrella still." She pulled up the seat to reveal a compartment containing a pair of bright orange rain pants and a hooded poncho. She slipped into them while I shielded her from the worst of the blast. Then she gave me a peck on the cheek and puttered away, sitting obstinately upright in the face of the storm.

The storm had passed and the sky was beginning to clear by the time Parkinson showed up at the warehouse. He asked me to go with him to take a look at Juice's place.

"Why?"

"You knew him as well as anybody, excluding his wife, and I thought you might see something we missed."

"Did you find the suitcases?"

"No."

"You still think they might be at his house?"

"We're reasonably sure they're not."

"Then what're you looking for?"

"If we knew that, we wouldn't need your help."

On the way over, he added, "We're pulling off your surveillance."

"Now?"

"That's right."

"What about the Deejay and the Shooter?"

"There's been no sign of them since Saturday, and the captain thinks we scared them off."

"What do *you* think?"

"What *I* think doesn't matter. We have a rapist hitting the Medical Branch area and a string of burglaries on Seawall, and we don't have enough personnel to go around. Your house is on the list for an hourly drive-by, but that's the best I can do."

I wasn't happy about it, and I had a hunch that Parkinson wasn't either. But he made it clear that, like it or not, this was the way it was going to be.

Juice collected things. Not stamps or coins or first editions, just things, anything that struck his fancy. His collection had grown since I'd last visited, overflowing the house to fill the garage and cover half the length of the driveway, so his two cars—a primer-coated '55 Ford and a beat-up Austin-Healy—had to be parked in the yard. The leased canary yellow Lincoln Town Car he'd driven to the warehouse the night he was killed had been impounded by the police.

Inside the house was even worse. Lorene had never been a neatness freak, but she had occasionally gone on cleaning binges. Juice had binges, too, but they didn't run in the same vein. The front door was blocked from inside, so we went around to the back and climbed the stairs to the rear deck.

The kitchen was neater than I'd ever seen it, but Parkinson explained that his people had done the dishes and taken out the trash. "Purely in self-defense," he assured me. "The stink was driving them out of the house."

The living room was packed to capacity. The windows were blocked by stacks of boxes, but a bare bulb in the middle of the ceiling revealed the details of Juice's obsession. I counted four jukeboxes and three exercise bikes (never used, I'm sure, at least not by Juice), a shoulder-high white Styrofoam sculpture of a man's head, an extensive selection of road signs, the grille from an Edsel, boxes of madras shirts, assorted matchbooks, baseball cards, souvenirs (such as an ashtray in the shape of a miniature toilet, captioned 'The *Butt* stops here!'), and magazines, thousands of them, cresting head-high against the wall to the left and washing over the room like a tide. There was also an expensive collection of records and tapes and the hardware needed to play them, but none of it could be reached except by mountaineering.

"Find anything interesting?" I asked.

"Your friend had the most comprehensive collection of print pornography I've ever examined."

"You examined it?"

"Briefly," he said. "I'm a busy man."

"Is the rest of the house like this?"

"Worse. I don't know where he slept."

"On a recliner in front of the TV."

"What recliner?"

I pointed toward the far corner of the living room. "See the floor lamp?"

"Which one?"

"With the gold tassels."

"Yeah."

"The recliner's underneath it . . . I think."

He stood on his toes, then shook his head and glanced through his list. "Let's see . . . Ummm. Here it is. One La-Z-Boy recliner. And . . . *six* televisions, one in operation when the premises was entered."

"He never turned it off. Juice had a theory that turning things off made them break down. I suppose that made sense to somebody who'd always had trouble starting and stopping."

"You want to see the rest?"

"Not really."

"Come on." Edging sideways down the hall, he asked, "Why did he need over a hundred rolls of toilet paper?"

"He hated running out of things, so he bought them by the gross. More expensive items, he purchased in pairs. You noticed the two cars out front."

"Yeah, but neither of them *runs*."

The bathroom stank of piss and mildew, but Parkinson insisted I take a good look. There wasn't much to see. A toothbrush and a squashed tube of Crest. A matching set of Brut cologne, aftershave, and deodorant. A Remington microscreen razor. A pile of towels in one corner, fungus growing in the others. And a bathtub ring like an alien sunset, in green and brown and gray. I didn't see any clues.

After we had peeked into all the rooms, Parkinson led me down to the basement. Because of the danger of flooding, few houses in Galveston had basements. In this case, extra dirt had been brought in and graded to form a steep slope up to the front of the house, and the basement was actually at ground level.

As we started down the stairs, the phone rang, and Parkinson went back up to answer it. I headed on down and worked my way between stacks of boxes to the far wall. Lorene hadn't approved of Juice smoking dope, so he'd kept it down here. He'd loosened a concrete block near floor level, split it in half, and hid his personal stash behind it. Of course, the smell would always drift up into the house, and they'd get into screaming fights over it later. But it hadn't stopped Juice, or stopped me from joining him.

There was a full ounce in place, and I considered the matter all of two seconds before stuffing the bag into my sock. I reasoned that Juice wouldn't be smoking it, and if anyone had a just claim of inheritance it was me. Lorene was welcome to the house and contents, but Juice would have wanted me to have his pot.

When Parkinson reappeared, he asked, "Find anything?"

"Nothing significant."

"You hungry?"

"I could eat something."

"I'm buying."

He broke a ten at Popeye's on spicy fried chicken and Cajun rice.

"Did you notice anything?" he asked.

"I didn't know his pack-rat obsession had gotten so bad. Most of that stuff wasn't there the last time I visited."

"When was that?"

"Maybe three months ago . . . before Lorene left him."

"See a relationship?"

"Between what and what?"

"Between being abandoned by his friends and the condition of his house."

"You mean he tried to fill the void with madras shirts and canned goods?"

He shrugged. "Notice anything else?"

"I didn't know what to look for."

"What about something you *didn't* notice?" When I gave him a blank stare, he asked, "Was there anything you expected to see that you didn't?"

"I don't think so."

"I'm looking for something special, something he always kept with him."

"Like Linus and his blanket?"

"Yeah. What was Harvey's security blanket?"

Nothing came to mind.

"There has to be something," he said. "A picture of his mother, his father's watch . . . I don't know, something."

"Is the case going that badly?"

He lifted his shoulders and let them drop. "With a murder, you either solve it immediately or it takes longer. This one's taking longer." That was a joke, I think, though it wasn't always easy to tell with Parkinson. He sipped his iced tea. "You want to know what's frustrating?"

"What?"

"Except for you, we can't seem to find anybody who disliked the guy. Everybody we spoke to seemed to think well of him. He was variously described as 'a barrel of laughs,' 'a really generous guy,' and 'a hell of a human being.' Nobody else used terms like 'slob' or 'liar.'"

"I imagine none of those people had him stealing from them."

"True," he agreed. "Which brings us to the most frustrating part of all. The motive. Except for you, nobody seems to have one."

"Are you telling me *I'm* your prime suspect?"

58

"Frustrating, isn't it?"

"You know, if I *had* killed Juice—which I didn't—I might be reluctant to reveal my true feelings. So maybe you should be talking to those people who called him a barrel of laughs or a hell of a human being."

"We don't necessarily assume people always tell us the truth," he said dryly. "But you should keep thinking about Harvey's security blanket. It might take a little pressure off you."

"What about his scrapbook?"

"What scrapbook?"

"*The* scrapbook. A fat one. It was nearly a foot thick when he retired from baseball."

Parkinson glanced through his list of household contents. "No scrapbook listed."

"It took a lot to get Juice mad, but the maddest I ever saw him was one time in the minors when Butch Sutton stole his scrapbook. Butch beat the crap out of Juice. But nobody ever touched his scrapbook after that."

Parkinson looked interested.

"Does that help?" I asked.

"It might."

"How?"

"Find the scrapbook, and maybe we'll find the suitcases."

CHAPTER 11

I headed home after work, took one look at my house, and decided I didn't want to go in there. Not tonight. Not without police protection. It was still daylight, not even 6:30, but darkness was already peeking out of the windows. I thought about running out and buying a gun, but I didn't like guns and didn't really know how to use one. Hadn't even fired a rifle in nearly twenty years. So, instead of arming myself, I went out for dinner and spent the evening prowling Juice's old haunts, buying rounds for his good buddies. I suppose I was looking for something—answers probably—but mostly I just wanted people around me.

I was pretty looped by eleven and was about to call it a night when the name Phillie Dog Ruttenberg came up. Somebody said they'd seen him shooting pool at Mary's II, and I decided to check it out. Mary's II was a gay bar that attracted a few straight customers with its pool table. Since it was only a half-dozen blocks away, I left my pickup where it was and walked.

Phillie Dog was leaning on a cue stick, holding court for a

handful of sleepy drunks. He cut off his harangue when he spotted me and staggered over, listing to port, then starboard. The Dog was short, dark, and slight, looking like Al Pacino might look after six months of starvation. But what he lacked in stature he made up for in nervous energy. He was forty years old, of Central European descent, but had the dialect and physical mannerisms of a black ghetto teenager, always struttin', shuckin', and jivin'.

"Wha' say, my man. Gimme fi'." I did. "How 'bout that Juice gettin' shot up like that. Don't it just beat all shit? Who'da figured? Not me, I tell you. Not the Juicer. Sweeter guy you'd never wanna meet."

"How's it hangin', Dog?"

"Steppin' all over it," he said, and cackled. "Grab a cue."

While racking the balls, I asked if he had any idea who might have wanted to kill Juice.

"He was into Rufus Jones for a grand, but he told me it was tooken care of. And Jones would'na left without he was paid."

"You sure he's gone?"

"No question. Hard to hide that Indian."

"When'd they leave?"

"Been three four weeks now. Gone to Vegas, 'Lannic City, one those places." He carefully lined up the break, reared back, and flipped the cue ball halfway across the room.

I recovered it for him. "Can you think of anybody else who'd have a reason to kill Juice?"

"Nah," he insisted. "Everybody like the Juicer. Even that fat fuck, Jones. Told me so hisself."

I played out the game, bought him a beer, and left. A gust of hot wind hit me as I stepped outside, and I saw a bank of clouds moving in from the west. I started up the sidewalk walking reasonably straight but hearing that faint, high-pitched hum of inebriation.

As I neared the corner, I thought I heard something behind me, but I saw only empty sidewalk when I looked back. I was halfway down the next block when I heard something

61

moving on the other side of the tall hedge that bordered the sidewalk. I thought it was a dog at first, something big, like a German shepherd. But the sound cut off as I stopped, and my heart started to pound. I couldn't see anything through the foliage, but I knew I wasn't alone. There was a gap in the hedge just ahead, and I also knew I'd never be able to walk past it.

It wasn't even midnight yet, but the street was deserted, all the houses dark and shut up. Where was everybody?

I backed across the street, heart drumming in my ears, eyes glued to the gap in the hedge. When a shadow stepped in to fill it, I ran. I couldn't help it; it wasn't a matter of choice. My body turned under its own volition and bolted.

I covered two blocks like I'd been shot from a cannon, then stopped, winded, and looked back. Blinding light hit me as I turned, and I let out a terrified yelp as I dropped to the pavement.

Then a car materialized out of the glare, with a little boy's grinning face pressed to the window. And I suddenly felt like an idiot.

What the hell's wrong with you? You think you see a shadow, and you go ape. Get a grip on yourself!

I got up and dusted myself off, took a deep breath, and let it out slowly as I walked on. I walked fast but managed to resist breaking into a run, staying on the road to avoid the shadows. When I reached the pickup, I took a slow lap around it from a safe distance before walking up close enough to check out the bed and the cab. Feeling a little foolish, I even peeked underneath. Then I climbed in, drove down to Seawall, and took a hotel room for the night.

I spent Tuesday morning inventorying the contents of two houses and was back in the office working on the estimates when Parkinson dropped by to report on progress.

"No scrapbook or suitcases," he said, "but we have uncovered some interesting facts."

"Such as?"

"In September of 'seventy-nine, Hanzlik traveled to Guatemala and the Yucatan peninsula as a bodyguard for Julius Brauer. He came back about a week earlier than his employer and deposited ten thousand in his bank account shortly after his return. He added another ten thousand during the next two months. Then he withdrew the twenty from his account in the first week of January and made a second trip to Guatemala, this time on his own. During the month following his return, he made two deposits totaling fifty thousand dollars. He made a third trip to Guatemala in February and deposited another fifty thousand in his account during the next month, the bulk of which he claimed to have realized from the sale of coin and stamp collections inherited from his grandfather. But his mother doesn't remember those collections, and there was no mention of them in the grandfather's will. The fact is, nobody seems to know where he got the hundred grand."

"That was the money he invested in the warehouse?"

"Most of it. He also borrowed five thousand from Mrs. Boatman and sold off a few assets for the rest."

"So, you figure he was dealing drugs?"

"That's the prevailing theory."

"It would be."

"Have any other ideas?"

"Not offhand."

"He never told you about those trips?"

"I remember some humorous anecdotes about working for Julie, but I don't think there was any mention of drugs being involved."

"Think about it. Maybe you'll remember something."

"Okay."

"Also, I'd like you to make a list of all the places where Hanzlik stayed while you've been on the island. I'm looking for places where he wouldn't have paid rent, where there would have been no record—places he liked to visit and people he might have stayed with even a night or two."

"I'll work on it."

"Good. We'll pick up the list this evening."

*　　*　　*

Molly rang my doorbell just after seven, looking delectable in tight jeans and a green silk blouse. I let her in, and she followed me back to the kitchen.

"Whatcha cooking?"

"Filets of sole à la Cochran."

"Smells great."

"It's classic French, minus the heavy cream and cognac."

"Do you give out recipes?"

"Only in special cases."

"Please."

When she fluttered her lashes, I decided this was a special case. "It's simple, really. Filets of sole, shallots, tomatoes, parsley, butter, and enough white vermouth to cover it. I'll write it down for you."

"My mouth's watering already."

"Tastes even better than it sounds."

After dinner, we retired to the study.

She looked around, surveying my renovations, and asked, "You did *this*?"

I insisted with becoming modesty, "Nothing to it."

We sat in the red leather chairs framing the hearth, me sipping the warm remains of my first glass of wine, Molly working on her third.

"Don't drink much, do you?" she asked.

"I have other vices."

She chuckled. "Yeah, I know. Chin smelled the pot last night."

"You people don't miss much."

"Marijuana is against the law, you know."

"Is it? Silly old law."

"Do you only obey those you approve of?"

"Sure. Doesn't everybody?"

She smiled, and time passed, a comfortable silence stretching between us. We sat slouched in our chairs, knees almost touching, listening to some Debussy on my CD player. Her eyes occasionally caught mine over the rim of her glass, her glance more curious than teasing. She was careful, and I could appreciate that.

She grinned. "I like you, too."

I laughed. "Is having your mind read one of the hazards of a relationship with a detective?"

"Are we having a relationship?"

"Not yet."

"But you have hope?"

"Can't deny me that."

She smiled. "How'd you remain single so long?"

"Wasn't easy. How about you?"

"Nobody wants a cop except another cop."

"I beg to differ."

She laughed. "I enjoy fencing with you, Bill. But"—she retracted her knees and sat up—"I really *don't* date suspects."

"Then we're going to have to stop meeting like this."

She sighed. "You're probably right. Call it an unwise attempt to mix business with pleasure."

"This is *business*?"

"That was my excuse," she said. "The lieutenant asked me to pick up the list of the places where Harvey stayed on the island."

I fetched it from the desk. "So, I'm still a suspect?"

"Lieutenant Parkinson doesn't think so."

That was news to me. "And you?"

"I don't think we know enough to start eliminating suspects."

"Why not?"

"Too many missing pieces." She put down her glass and leaned in to tackle the problem. "Take a look at it: Harvey gets two suitcases from somewhere. He's supposed to deliver them to the Deejay but tells him they're lost in the warehouse."

"But they *aren't*."

"Then he was lying."

"You mean the suitcases were never there?"

"Or they *were,* and he removed them."

"Why would he do that?"

"Maybe he wanted more for them than the Deejay was offering. Or maybe he was convinced the Deejay was going to kill him and hid the suitcases to protect himself."

"But they killed him anyway."

"Because the Deejay believed he could get the suitcases from *you*."

"So, where are they?"

"That's what we're hoping you can tell us."

"A vain hope, I'm afraid. Besides, there's one thing wrong with your scenario."

"What's that?"

"When I saw Juice last Wednesday, he didn't know where the suitcases were. And he couldn't have moved them if he couldn't find them."

"Maybe he found them later."

"Maybe. But he wasn't at the warehouse on Thursday or Friday during the day, and to enter at night he'd have had to turn off the alarm and call the security company. So they'd have a record."

She nodded and consulted her notes. "He turned it off on Friday evening at ten-oh-five. That was over an hour before he called you, and he could have spent the time looking for the suitcases."

"If he found them, why was he so scared?"

"I don't know," she admitted. "And if he found them, they should have been in the warehouse."

"But what if he *didn't* find them? What if somebody else took them out of the box?"

"Who?"

"I don't know."

"It would almost have to be an inside job."

"Meaning one of my regulars?"

"Who else would have had access to the boxes?"

"Maybe one of the drivers."

"We'll need a list."

"Okay."

"If it *was* one of your regulars, which would it be?"

"Christ! I don't even want to think about it."

66

"Tony Perelli?"

"No. I don't believe it."

"His family was Mafia."

"*Was*. That was thirty years ago. Tony's ashamed of all that, doesn't even like to talk about it. And I really can't see him being part of this."

"What about Santiago?"

"What about him?"

"He has a sheet. Did time in Arizona for car theft."

"I didn't know that. But he's a good worker. I have no complaints."

She shrugged. "He seems a likely suspect."

"Because he's an ex-con?"

"Of course."

"I hope you're wrong."

"How long has he worked for you?"

"Since 'eighty-three."

"Legrange Taylor also has a sheet, you know?"

"Yeah, Leggy told me. Said he did hard labor for breaking and entering. But that was a long time ago."

"Thirty years," she agreed. "And he's been clean since then, as far as we know. How close was he to Harvey?"

"They liked each other, went out drinking or fishing together. Leggy and Tony've been with us from the beginning, and I can't believe either of them would have anything to do with killing Juice."

"What do you think of Randy Oliver?"

"I like him."

"Think he could be involved in this?"

"No, I can't see it. He's a good kid."

"Would you call him naive?"

"I suppose so."

"Then he might be tricked into doing something illegal."

"Maybe, but I doubt he'd be able to keep it secret. Besides, he's a summer worker, only been with us a little over a month."

67

She slipped her notebook into her purse and came to her feet. "Well, now that I've jeopardized your trust in all your friends and associates, I'll take my leave."

"Do you have to?"

"No." She examined me for a moment and smiled. "But I think I'd better."

CHAPTER 12

I drove out to Gareth's place Wednesday evening. It was off Stewart Road beyond the western end of the seawall: twenty inland acres of sedge and Bermuda grass, live oak and transplanted palms, with the driveway and property boundaries marked by white paddock fencing. He stabled a half-dozen horses in a cement-block barn and had a pool and a roomy brick ranch house built for comfort instead of show.

I parked behind Gareth's silver Porsche and climbed out as he appeared in swimming trunks and flipflops, beach towel draped jauntily over his shoulder.

"Care for a swim?" he asked.

"Didn't bring my trunks."

"I promise not to look."

"What about Syb?"

"She'd love a peek. Should I call her?"

I took off my clothes behind one of the fat oleander bushes that screened the pool, then hit the water at a sprint.

When we were both afloat, I asked, "How were the islands?"

"Surrounded by water."

"No kidding."

"Trust me."

"Isn't it hot down there this time of year?"

"That's the way Syb likes it."

"That's what I hear."

When she appeared with two king-size frozen margaritas, he said, "Hide your eyes, love. Bull is buck nekkid and feelin' shy."

"I trust you explained that, as a former nurse, I've seen my share of pee-pees."

"Not like his, you haven't. They don't call him Bull for nothin'."

She smiled tolerantly. "Dinner's ready when you are."

Sunset was gilding the landscape as we carried our glasses up to the house. Sybil was waiting with refills and nachos, followed by chili, tamales, and guacamole. The chili was made with pinto beans—which many Texans considered a sacrilege, but I happened to like—stew-size chunks of beef, hot jalapeños, and lots of chili powder.

"Terrific," I told Sybil.

"Not too spicy?"

"Just right."

"You're sweating," Gareth pointed out.

"A good excuse for more margaritas."

"Not tonight," he insisted. "Two's your limit. Margaritas are too sweet for serious drinking. For that, I thought we'd move on to Foster's. Syb! Bring on the lager!"

It was the live-in cook/housekeeper's evening off, and Sybil was good-humoredly acting as her stand-in.

We sipped our Foster's straight from the oversized 25-ounce cans. After the first round, we retired to the living room, and I discovered that the floor had developed irregularities I hadn't noticed on the way in.

Gareth plopped on a sofa. "Where's your beer? Syb! We're dry in here!"

She supplied fresh cans, and Gareth raised his. "To Harvey Nathan 'Juice' Hanzlik, a gentle man in an ungentle world."

"Yeah. Ole Juice."

Gareth chuckled. "Remember that time we took him out on the *Lida Rose,* and—"

"And he was sick all day?"

"*Sick?* I've never seen so much vomit."

"It was that huge breakfast he had."

"Half-digested hotcakes and syrup and eggs and bacon—"

"Everywhere!"

"But he kept us laughing."

"When he wasn't upchucking his lungs."

"Wouldn't let us bring him in, though. Oh, no! Didn't mind ruining my deck and brightwork, but—"

"But he wouldn't let us spoil our day."

Gareth wiped his eyes. "He loved you, you know?"

"Who?"

"Who the hell're we talkin' about? How many dead friends do you have?"

"Only one. So far."

"He loved you."

"He tol' you that?"

"He did."

"Ole Juice." I was starting to get a little misty-eyed. "He was the only thing that made being in the minors tolberal . . . toleradal . . . possible."

When Gareth got drunk enough, he suddenly burst into song. He wailed out an old Welsh air about a fair lad who died fighting the British, then followed it with several other maudlin paeans to death and glory. I even joined in on the choruses of "Tom Dooley" and "The Ballad of Wyatt Earp."

Tears rolling down my face, I said, "He needed my help . . ."

"Who?"

". . . and I didn't do anything."

"You didn't know."

"I didn't even try."

"Ya mustn't blame yerself."

"Jus' turned him off . . . wouldn't even listen to him."

He patted my shoulder. "It's all right, Bull."

But even in my condition, I knew it *wasn't.* Juice was the best friend I'd ever had, and I had failed him miserably.

CHAPTER 13

During the lunch break on Thursday, Leggy talked me into showing Randy my fastball. I hadn't thrown in six months and didn't really feel up to it. But Leggy badgered me into doing a little soft tossing, and we gradually worked our way back to sixty feet, six inches.

Juice had marked off the distance against the side of the dock with bold strokes of Day-Glo yellow back when we first bought the place. We had even created a mound and a home plate out near the fence away from the dock. We hadn't used it in a long time, and the rain and traffic had worn down the mound. But the brick we had sunk in the dirt for a rubber was still there, so I could get a fair pushoff.

The cowhide felt good in my hand, the ridged seams forming familiar terrain. I was stiff and sluggish at first, but my muscles responded to the heat, and my arm felt pretty loose after about ten minutes of throwing.

I had to talk myself through the windup at first, recreating it step by step: rock, toe, rock, plant, kick, coil, drive, plant, release, and follow through. But my instinct took over as I found my rhythm.

Leggy was using an old catcher's mitt of Juice's with a deep pocket that didn't offer much protection. The first time I aired one out, he tore off the glove and hopped around blowing on his hand. After the second, he went into the warehouse and found some cardboard to stuff into the mitt.

I concentrated on keeping the motion fluid and settled in at about three-quarter velocity. But I was getting pretty good pop on the ball and may have thrown a couple in the middle eighties.

It was an art form I had practiced for over twenty years, and I was relieved I hadn't entirely lost the touch. The equipment needed maintenance, but it still worked. Once or twice I even got a taste of the old power, that electrical charge of invincibility, feeling like Zeus hurling thunderbolts. The charge was pretty low voltage, but it brought back memories.

They were a mixed bag, as you'd expect—some good, some bad. Exhilaration was there and triumph but also much disappointment and considerable embarrassment. You don't know what the word means until you've made a complete ass of yourself in front of thirty thousand people.

When I called it a day, Randy told me respectfully, "You were throwin' smoke, sir."

And Leggy allowed, "Mighty hard on the hand but awesome to behold."

I tried not to show it, but I was soaking this up like a sponge.

Parkinson came by an hour later and asked me to go with him to see Anna Mae Boatman.

"With older people," he explained, "I find it easier to work with an intermediary, somebody they know and trust."

Anna Mae lived in a storm-shuttered bungalow a few blocks from the beach, with a neatly trimmed hedge and two transplanted palm trees out front and her red scooter sitting in the driveway.

"Three times in the same week!" she cried when she opened the door. "You expectin' me to die soon?"

I introduced Parkinson, and he offered his hand. "It's a pleasure to meet you, Mrs. Boatman."

She ignored the hand. "You the one in charge of Harvey's murder?"

"I'm directing the investigation, yes, ma'am."

"Where are the ones that did it?" she asked. "That's what I want to know. Why aren't they in irons? You tell me that."

"Well . . ."

"It's barbaric," she declared. "A respectable citizen killed in broad daylight."

He tried to explain that it had actually taken place after midnight, but she wasn't interested in details. She wanted results.

"Harvey may have been absent the day they handed out brains," she said, "but dumb ain't a crime or the jails'd all be full. So you find the people that did it. You hear?"

Parkinson did his Jack Webb. "Yes, ma'am."

"If not, you'll answer to me."

"Yes, ma'am."

"Don't want that, do you?"

"No, ma'am."

She nodded and smiled at both of us. "Well, don't just stand there lettin' in the heat. Come on in and have some lemonade."

The lemonade was tart and icy and hit the spot.

When we were all seated, glasses in hand, Anna Mae turned to Parkinson. "So you've come to ask me about Harvey?"

"Yes, ma'am."

"How can I help?"

"When did you last see him?"

"Last Thursday afternoon. I was trimmin' the hedge when he drove up."

"What time was that?"

"I'd say about eleven o'clock."

"How long did he stay?"

"Couple of hours."

74

"Did he seem nervous?"

"Like a fly in a bottle."

"Did he say why?"

"Didn't wanna talk about it. Wouldn't sit still. Didn't even eat his pineapple upside-down cake. That's how I knew it was serious."

"Did he bring anything into the house with him?"

"Suitcases, you mean?" She was a sharp old woman. Even Parkinson had to smile. Then he glanced at me.

"I told her."

"Yes, ma'am," he said. "Did you see any suitcases?"

"No, sir, I didn't."

"Was he in your presence the whole time he was here?"

"No, sir. He had to answer nature's call at least once."

He suppressed another smile. Two in one day would have been inconceivable. "Could he have gone out to his car and reentered the house without your knowledge."

"Well, yes, sir. I'd have to say that was possible."

"Would you mind if we looked around?"

"Where?" She wasn't happy about having her sanctorum invaded.

"Any place he could have hidden the suitcases: closets, attic, basement, garage."

"Got no basement," she said, "and I don't think he went up to the attic."

"Do you mind if we check?"

"I guess not," she decided. "Anything to help you find Harvey's murderers. But you just be sure to catch 'em, you hear?"

"Yes, ma'am, I hear."

We found two suitcases in a bedroom closet (American Tourister, not Samsonite) and two trunks in the attic. The garage contained a lawn mower, a coil of garden hose, and various tools hung neatly on pegs. At the back was an ancient console television and a chest freezer. The freezer was locked.

"Freezer?" asked Anna Mae. "I haven't used that thing in years."

"It's locked, ma'am."

"Isn't the key in it?"

"No, ma'am."

"Well, it *was*."

"Do you mind if we send for a locksmith?"

She didn't mind, and the freezer was opened.

It contained several dead palmetto bugs but no suitcases or scrapbook.

CHAPTER 14

Suffering another attack of anxiety, I spent Thursday night at the old Galvez Hotel, a bit of nineteenth-century Mediterranean elegance overlooking the gulf. When I arrived at work the next morning, I found a message to call Parkinson waiting for me.

"Do you know Conchita Juarez?" he asked.

"I know she and Juice had something going at one time. I told Detective Flanagan about her."

"She says she has Hanzlik's scrapbook, but she'll only give it to you."

"*Me?* I hardly know her."

"Will you go with me to see her?"

"I have a business to run, you know."

"We'd like to see that scrapbook."

"I understand that, but we're busy here today, and I have deliveries to make."

"Shouldn't take long."

I sighed.

"Good," he said. "Pick you up in ten minutes."

Conchita Juarez lived on a potholed stretch of Avenue E across from the freight yards. The house was a white concrete-block box built on a half lot with a tiny bare earth yard in front scattered with toys. The place wasn't much, but Conchita was making the best of it. The paint job was fresh, the red shutters glaring in the sunlight. Sunflowers and petunias were planted in boxes on both sides of the door. A dusty mixed-breed dog was urinating on the petunias, but they were holding their own so far. Two boys, one about ten, the other maybe a year younger, both skinny and shirtless, were tossing a baseball in the street. And a little girl squatted bare-ass in the dirt, digging a hole with a GI Joe.

Conchita opened the door before we got to it and ushered us into the living room, which was pleasantly cool, thanks to a big window unit. The orange walls and velvet paintings weren't to my taste, but the room was clean and tidy. Smelling Lemon Pledge and recently disturbed dust, I assumed the tidiness was in our honor.

Conchita was an attractive woman in her late thirties. She was a few pounds heavier than I remembered but big enough to carry it. With her large breasts, satiny skin, and heavy black hair, she was a sort of younger, Hispanic version of Juice's mother.

When Parkinson and I were seated, she said, "Harbey ask me to gib you something. He told me I must only gib it to you."

I nodded.

She told Parkinson, "You stay."

"Yes, ma'am."

She crooked a finger at me and sashayed out of the room with a wonderfully liquid motion of her hips, leading me down a short hall into a room barely big enough for a bed, a dresser, and a polished cedar chest. Inside the chest among her other treasures lay Juice's scrapbook.

"Please," she said. "It is berry hebby."

She wasn't kidding. The thing was at least a foot thick and must have weighed fifteen to twenty pounds. It was the usual dime store photo album with black vinyl-over-cardboard covers, the sort often held together with ribbons. But this one had grown far beyond the strength of ribbons or even rawhide thongs and was lashed together with stout wire.

When tears welled up in Conchita's eyes, I didn't know what to do. Since she looked like she needed a hug, I gave her one. And she held on tightly, needing it more than I'd realized.

"He was good to me," she said.

"I'm sure he was."

"He loved you."

"I know." It appeared to be common knowledge.

Eyes brimming, she said, "You must help them."

"Them?"

"The police. You must help them find the ones who did this."

I wasn't sure what she expected me to do, but I promised to do my best.

After she'd had her cry and straightened her face, we went back to the living room.

Parkinson stood. "When did Mr. Hanzlik give you the scrapbook, Mrs. Juarez?"

"Thursday ebening."

"Did he spend the night?"

She looked away. "Yes."

"Did he tell you he was in trouble?"

"He say he might not come back."

"Did he say why?"

She shook her head.

"Did you ask him?"

"He not want to talk about it."

"Did he mention any names?"

She glanced at me. "Only him. Harbey say I must gib him the book."

"One last question," Parkinson said. "Why did you wait so long to tell anyone you had the scrapbook?"

She dropped her eyes. "I did not want to know."

"Know?"

Her chin trembled. "That Harbey is dead."

He nodded and said quietly, "Thank you."

She turned to me. "You want coffee?"

"We don't want to put you to any trouble."

"I hab only to get it."

I caught Parkinson's eye, and he shrugged.

"Then, yes," I said. "Please."

The coffee was very hot and very strong. She stood and watched us drink every drop, then took the cups and escorted us to the door.

I went home that evening to change, then drove out to Cleary's for some seafood. After dinner, I found another hotel room for the night. I tried to watch a pay movie, but I couldn't keep my mind on it.

Conchita had started me thinking that maybe I should *do* something. I knew a restaurant hostess wasn't necessarily an authority on such matters, but the police weren't making much progress, and I thought that maybe I could . . . Could what?

I've always been a sucker for thrillers in which seemingly ordinary people solve cases that have left major police organizations baffled. But the fact that I enjoyed reading such stories didn't necessarily mean I *believed* them. On the other hand, my best friend had been killed, and his last act had been an effort to save my life—"No! Not him!"—and it seemed only appropriate that I should take a personal interest in seeing his murderers brought to justice.

But if I decided to do something, I had the problem of deciding *what* I should do. I knew nothing about solving crimes. And, unlike the police, I had no established sources of information. So, where should I start?

Saturday was slow at the warehouse, and I let Tony run things while I spent the day at my desk attempting to concoct an investigative strategy. I bought a pocket-size spiral-ring notebook and began by jotting down possible leads, potential suspects, and so on. But, in spite of all the Dick Francis, Elmore

80

Leonard, and Lawrence Sanders I'd read, the harvest was meager.

I knew a real detective would probably start by talking to Juice's mother and his widow, but I'd had all of Barbara Sue and Lorene I could stand. So I decided to approach the problem from the other end.

If, as we assumed, someone other than Juice had taken the suitcases out of the warehouse, there had to be an inside man. I made a list of likely suspects, which was of course the same list I had given the police: all warehouse personnel and the drivers I'd worked with during the past year. After some thought, I tentatively eliminated the part-timers and drivers, deciding to concentrate on the regulars simply because they had the most access to the warehouse.

I knew Tony the best, and I couldn't picture him doing anything criminal. Number one, because Jesus wouldn't like it; and, two, because he would be set up quite comfortably when his uncle died, so he had the most to lose from getting caught. I liked Leggy too much to seriously consider him a suspect, and I figured his staying clean for thirty years had earned him the benefit of the doubt. As for Randy? Give me a break.

Of the regulars, that left only Mariano. The police had considered him a prime suspect, and I could see their point. It wasn't only his record; it was his persona. There was something undeniably dangerous about Mariano. And, though we had worked together for six years, I really didn't know much about him. I knew he was a reliable worker, shot a mean game of pool, and had a good head for beer, but that didn't tell me *who he was*. And I figured it was time I made an effort to find out.

That took care of the inside man, but what about the one on the outside? If drugs were involved, somebody had to front the cash. In which case, I was also looking for an individual who could lay hands on a quick fifty to a hundred thousand dollars.

I made another list, putting Julie Brauer at the top. It made sense. He had money and knew Juice. He was already in trouble with the law and was known to use drugs, especially cocaine. And, most important, I didn't like him.

The list also included a few restaurant owners and real estate mavens of Juice's acquaintance. And I reluctantly added Gareth and Anna Mae. I didn't believe either was involved, but they fit the criteria: they were friends of Juice's, and they might be able to come up with the cash.

CHAPTER 15

I planned to start my snooping on Monday, but Sunday was my day of rest. It was also, by charming coincidence, Molly Flanagan's day off, and she generously consented to spend it with me. At noon, we met at Guido's for crab claws and Bloody Marys, then went for a stroll along the seawall.

The sea hates the land. She divides to conquer, and barrier islands are her spoils of victory. Galveston was ripped from the belly of Texas thousands of years ago and has suffered continual abuse ever since, perpetually being built up, torn down, and reshaped by the gulf. The hurricane of 1900 washed away three hundred feet of the island and killed six thousand people in an era when shore development was just beginning, and construction on the Galveston Seawall was begun in 1902 in an effort to prevent an even worse disaster.

Over the next sixty years, in five separate construction projects, the seaward side of the island was raised seventeen feet for a stretch of nearly ten miles, and a great wall of Texas granite was erected to blunt the waves. After the storm of 1915 swept away most of Galveston's wide beaches, construction was started on a system of thirteen groins between 12th and 59th Streets, fingers of stone that jutted five hundred feet into the gulf. They were intended to protect the toe of the seawall and to prevent further beach erosion, but they had lived up to only the first half of their billing. Even with periodic loads of replacement sand, the beaches were now fifty feet at their widest, and the Army Corps of Engineers had estimated that it would take over fifty billion cubic yards of sand to return them to their original state.

However, on that bright hot Sunday afternoon, it wasn't the Galveston beaches that concerned me. It was Molly who had my undivided attention. Dressed in sandals, white shorts, and a striped top, there was considerably more of her to see than usual. And there was nothing on display I didn't like.

I liked the way she moved—an athletic, balls of the feet kind of swagger. I'd never noticed it before and wondered if she reserved it for her days off. I liked the way her body moved with her—breasts bobbing beneath her top, muscles flexing in her calves and thighs and buttocks (I had to drift back a bit for that view).

We ended our stroll at Stewart Beach Park, the biggest commercial beach and the best sand on the island. It began east of 12th Street, beyond the groins, and was maintained with regular loads of replacement sand.

Molly and I rode the Sky Rapids, played Mini Golf, clashed at Bumper Boats, and raced Speedway Go-Carts. Then we bought lemon Icees and rented two umbrella-shaded lounge chairs on the beach. For conversation, we stuck to personal stuff, barely mentioning the case. I even told her about my novel, the one I'd been working on periodically for ten years. She was the first person on the island I had discussed it with, except for Juice, of course.

Sitting on the beach, where I'd sat with him so many Sunday afternoons, triggered memories of all the good times we'd had. Juice'd had a knack for enjoying life, and it was hard not to enjoy it with him. Nothing seemed to bother him. I knew that was a deception, but his talent for finding a laugh in even the

84

most depressing situation was genuine. I used to laugh with him, but somewhere along the line I had stopped.

From what I could remember, the change had come gradually. My failure to make it in the Majors had done more damage to my ego than I was willing to admit, and Juice was a constant reminder. He'd had his disappointments, of course, but he'd never had my expectations. Somebody like him could never understand my feelings. That's what I told myself. His jokes had started to grate on me, and I'd allowed myself to believe he simply didn't care. Didn't care about anything. Too stupid to care.

But that was a lie. In spite of what Anna Mae had said, Juice wasn't dumb. He was limited: the only books I'd ever seen him read were the Bible and *Dianetics*. He had no education to speak of: high school hadn't made much intellectual impact, and he'd lasted only a year in junior college. He could also be awfully gullible, but it wasn't because he was blind to reality. It was selective vision. If you were his friend, you could do no wrong, and he would do anything for you. I had never really understood that kind of unquestioning loyalty, but I knew I was going to miss having that kind of friend.

Juice had played the clown so convincingly that it was easy to forget there was anything behind it. But I knew his buffoonery had shielded a surprisingly sensitive nature, just as his perpetual partying had masked a craving for peace and solitude, a craving he had revealed to me one night not long after I had arrived in Galveston.

We were shooting pool and drinking beer at The Pirate, an after-hours place downtown, when he suddenly decided he wanted to show me why he'd chosen to live on the island. It was past three in the morning, and neither of us was in any condition to drive, but that didn't sway Juice. He drove down to Seawall and headed west, past the Galvez Hotel; past the red-brick Convention and Visitors Center; past the Flagship Hotel, a prefabricated salmon-pink box built on its own pier; past the Bunker, twin gun emplacements left over from World War II, before they were landscaped by the San Luis Hotel; past all the seafood restaurants and motels and fishing piers; past Sea-Arama and the end of the seawall, where the boulevard becomes a divided highway. We drove on and on, the gulf invisible off to our left, the beach houses dark at 3:30 in the morning, headlight tunnels leading the way.

I was half-dozing when I thought I saw a suit of armor to the left of the road. It was real, as I discovered the next morning, though Juice pretended he didn't know what I was talking about at the time. He turned off toward the gulf shortly afterward and made another turn or two before pulling into the carport of a beach house.

He went inside and came out with hot dogs and buns and coat hangers, then built an illegal fire on the beach. The buns were moldy, so we ended up eating the dogs directly off the coat hangers.

It was a splendid night, a full moon glimmering on the water, and we stayed till dawn. Juice said he was going to live there some day. The house belonged to Anna Mae, and she was going to leave it to him. He went on and on about how peaceful it was with just the sea and the sky, getting downright poetic about it. And, in memory, it was everything he said it was.

Molly was staring at me. "Where were you?"

"Where I think Juice may have hidden the suitcases."

She sat up. "Where?"

"Come on." I pulled her to her feet. "I'll tell you on the way."

The land was low and boggy beyond the end of the seawall. There were a few wind-shaped clumps of live oak on the inland side but nothing between us and the frontal dunes except sawgrass and cattails, tide pools, some scraggly bushes, and beach houses. Lots of beach houses. The last hurricane, in '83, had done a lot of damage out here. But both sides of the road were lined with precarious-looking structures perched on stilts, and more were going up all the time.

I kept my eyes glued to the left side of the road, knowing the suit of armor wasn't a figment of my imagination. But, after ten minutes or so, after passing through Sunny Beach, Pirates Beach, and Palm Beach, I was beginning to lose faith.

The houses cut off as we entered Galveston Island State Park, and Molly asked, "When was the last time you were out here?"

"I was only at the beach house once, that first time, seven years ago. Juice kept inviting me, but I kept finding reasons not to come."

The houses picked up again after two miles of parkland in a stretch called Jamaica Beach. I didn't remember the suit of armor being this far out. I was sure we'd missed it, or that it was no longer there, but I didn't tell Molly. After seven years, the house could have been torn down, but I didn't tell her that either.

"Do you remember it being this far out?"

"No. But I swear it's . . . *There!* See it?"

She smiled, pretending she'd never doubted me. "I see it."

The suit of armor was barely five feet tall and a tad rusty, but there it stood at the side of the road in front of a gray-shingled real estate office.

The first road led to a development of relatively new redwood A-frames, so we retreated to the highway and headed west again.

The next left was marked with a beach access sign. The road intersected with another road running parallel to the beach, and we tried the left branch first. When I didn't see the house I was looking for, we turned around and headed back across the access road.

Evidence of the Bust could be seen in the general rundown condition of the houses in this development. They seemed to get worse as we drove along, and Anna Mae's was the last on the left. It was separated from the rest by an empty lot next door and another across the street, both covered by the same waist-high weeds that surrounded the house. The carport fronted the street, its collapsed roof leaning drunkenly against the attached storage room, while the house was set toward the back of the lot, its roof mangy from missing shingles, its white-painted siding weathering toward gray.

87

We checked the storage room first, ducking under the tilted carport to find the door standing open. But it contained only spider webs, two six-packs of Dr. Pepper empties, a bald tire, and a stack of rotting wood-and-canvas deck chairs.

Wading through the high grass toward the house, we passed a tarpaulin-covered mound of building materials. I recalled that Juice had been planning to do some work out here during the spring, but it looked like he hadn't got around to it.

The house was up on stilts like all the others, with just a poured slab of concrete and a padlocked utility room at ground level. I ran back to the truck for a crowbar, but after prying off the lock, we found only a collapsed float toy and more spider webs inside.

The steps up to the platform looked dangerous, and the hand-rail looked even worse, so we hugged the wall as we climbed. The steps creaked and groaned, several twisting loosely under-foot, but we made it safely to the top.

One of the sliding glass doors had been shattered, the work of vandals or weather. The shag carpeting in the front room was soggy and decaying, and the only furniture was the melting ruins of a sofa. The appliances, counter, sink, and cabinets had all been removed. The bedrooms had also been stripped but contained evidence of use: a decaying blanket and an empty quart Blue Ribbon beer bottle in the first; a laceless tennis shoe, a full ashtray, and a few pornographic magazines in the second.

No gray Samsonite suitcases.

Afterward, we stood on the deck contemplating the gulf, which was green today, instead of its usual murky gray—a gently rippling emerald fabric scattered with glitter.

I snuck in a few peeks at Molly, who stood with legs parted, facing the sea breeze, red curls dancing.

Juice would have liked her. *I* certainly did. Just being with her made me feel good. First time I'd felt that way in years. At twenty, I'd never have believed I'd be saying it, but I hadn't been to bed, couch, floor, or car seat with a woman in six months. I had started to think that something had gone seriously wrong down there until Molly had come along to rekindle that familiar sweet ache of lust.

When she caught me looking, I said, "Why don't we come out here next weekend for a picnic?"

She smiled, green eyes picking up highlights from the gulf, then turned back into the wind. "I don't know if I can get off."

"Will you try?"

She tossed me a teasing glance. "I'll see what I can do."

We drove back to town and found a place to eat, then I took her home to bed.

Nope. Sorry. I lied. Molly had paperwork to do. So what I really did was deliver her to her car, then head back to my lonely, oversized, and perpetually unfinished home. I was still leery of spending the night there, but I was fed up with hotel rooms and badly needed to give my credit cards a rest.

CHAPTER 16

Monday morning, I went back to work and started detecting. I began with Mariano, asking him to help me with a small apartment move-out in the Medical Branch area.

It was a shabby little second-story place with cheap rickety furniture—a mover's nightmare. The chest of drawers was the worst of the lot, and I knew at a glance it would never make the move in one piece. It was an oversized monster made of plastic-veneered eighth-inch plywood, stuck together with a few stingy dollops of glue. Even after removing the attached mirror and pulling out all the drawers it still couldn't support its own weight. It was expanding and contracting like an accordion by the time we wrestled it down the stairs, and one side came loose in my hands before we got it into the truck.

But this wasn't the first time something like this had happened to me, and I always carried glue and C-clamps in the cab. So I sent Mariano up to fetch a few one-man items while I put the chest back together. Once it was clamped and glued, I wrapped it in padding and strapped it tightly, relieved we only had to move it across town.

We had everything packed into the truck by twelve, and I drove us to a virtually identical apartment house on 37th Street. Then we broke for lunch, carrying our bags to a scrap of shade in the complex's tiny patch of grass. Mariano took out a sandwich, an apple, and a can of Bud. The temperature was in the mid-nineties, and his bag had been in the cab, so I could imagine how hot that beer was. Never could stand warm beer myself, and hot beer was beyond my comprehension, but he sipped it like it was fresh out of the cooler.

Now that I had Mariano where I wanted him, I couldn't seem to get started. He was no help, of course, patiently chewing his sandwich, downing his beer, and occasionally blessing me with an incurious glance. I thought I saw him smile once, but I couldn't guess what had provoked it.

Finally, I cast fate to the wind and said, "Hell of a week, wasn't it?"

He nodded and took another bite of his sandwich.

"You never really got to know Juice, did you?"

He shook his head.

"That's too bad," I said.

He chewed.

"You know you're a bit of a mystery, don't you?"

He drank to that.

"I mean," I stumbled on, "we've worked together for six years now, and . . . I thought maybe we should—you know—try to get to know each other a little better."

He popped the last of his sandwich into his mouth, washed it down with the last of his simmering brew, and let out a satisfied belch.

"I don't even know where you're from," I said. When he went for his apple, I quickly rephrased it as a question. "Where *are* you from?"

He paused, apple suspended on the way to his mouth, and gave me that uninflected stare Sitting Bull must have given Custer. He said, "Out west," then filled his mouth with apple.

91

Sensing he didn't want to talk about his past, I was stymied. Truth was, I didn't know what to say. I couldn't very well just come out and ask if he'd killed Juice.

"I didn't kill him," he said. "Didn't have nothin' to do with it." He picked a piece of apple peel from between his front teeth and drawled, "That what you wanted to know?"

Caught red-handed, I could only admit, "Yeah, I guess that's what I was askin'. Sorry, Mariano. I didn't really think you did it, but the cops have been on my ass, and I—"

"S'awright," he said as he came to his feet. Then he nodded, turned, and sauntered out to the truck, chomping on his apple.

And that was it, the full extent of my first stab at detecting. Nick Charles would have choked on his martini.

But I didn't let it stop me. After work, I watched Mariano climb into his rusty Army surplus jeep, then followed him in my pickup.

I discovered that tailing somebody isn't as easy as it looks on the tube. Three blocks from the warehouse, I got caught behind a car at a red light, and Mariano was out of sight by the time it changed.

By sheer dumb luck, I spotted him again as I turned onto Broadway. He was half a block ahead, just tooling along, black hair flapping in the breeze. I ran a red light at 33rd Street and kept him in sight until I almost lost him again at 40th. He made a left, and I barely managed the turn in time to see him cut right onto Avenue L two blocks down. I closed the gap fast enough to see him turn left again at 42nd, but by the time I followed, he had vanished. Halfway down the block, I glanced into the alley as I passed and saw him backing his jeep through a gap in a hedge.

I pulled over to the curb, got out, and ran down the alley until I spotted him climbing the stairs at the back of a three-story white frame house. After watching him enter a room on the top floor, I went back to the pickup and thought about what I'd learned. Mariano was either visiting somebody or he had moved out of his trailer. That was interesting. I hung around for a few minutes, then decided I should take a look at his former home.

The Island Magic Trailer Court was on the other side of

Broadway, off 45th Street, just above the freight yards, an impoverished establishment with only about half the slots occupied. I had taken Mariano home a few times and recognized his dusty silver Airstream, with a tarpaulin rigged along one side to create a combination porch and carport.

As I came to a stop, a woman appeared at my window. She was big and craggy-faced, with broad shoulders and long black hair streaked with gray. "Help you?" she rasped in a voice lower than mine.

"Just dropped by to see Mariano."

"Ain' home."

I felt like I'd stumbled into a gypsy camp and wondered if everybody here spoke in the same abbreviations. "Guess I'll try again later. Thanks."

"S'awright."

So I pulled out of the park and went home. Right? Wrong. I'm the fellow who stuck it out for five and half years in the minors. Remember?

What I did was find a place to leave my pickup and head back to the park. It was dinner time, and many of the inhabitants were dining outside their trailers, but Mariano's unit was on the edge, and I figured I should be able to reach it without being observed. The trailers to either side of his looked deserted, and the gypsy lady wasn't in sight, so I climbed the chain-link fence and pressed against the front of the trailer. Then I peeked around the edge, saw the coast was clear, and crept up to the door.

I was reaching for the doorknob when it suddenly occurred to me that it might be locked. I hadn't thought of that.

The handle turned but the door stuck, and I told myself, *Of course it's locked, you idiot. Nobody leaves their doors unlocked these days.*

But when I gave the door a frustrated jerk, it popped open with a blood-curdling SKREEEEENCH! loud enough to alert everybody in the trailer park to my presence.

My first impulse was to get the hell out of there. Then I noticed that the door was warped and scarred around the latch and realized it had been jimmied open. That was significant

93

enough to warrant further investigation, so I resisted the temptation to run, stepped in, and pulled the door shut until it jammed, leaving an inch-wide gap. It was suffocatingly hot inside, and I was immediately pouring sweat.

I'd expected to find the messy evidence of a search, but the trailer was surprisingly tidy, everything in its place. No coffee cups or dirty glasses, no scattered magazines or newspapers, no stray socks or unanswered mail. Mariano didn't have much, but what he had was strictly squared away. The tiny kitchen area was spick-and-span. The miniature bathroom was spotless. The bed linen was clean, the bed made in military fashion. There were three books on a shelf over the bed: *Harper's Anthology of Native American Poetry, The Complete Oxford Shakespeare,* and André Malraux's *Man's Fate.* Over the foot of the bed was a framed photograph of a woman: attractive, Asian, smiling seductively. There were two drawers built into the bedframe: one was empty; the other contained three 18 × 12 sketchpads.

They were filled with pencil and charcoal drawings: Western landscapes, men on horseback, buttes and plains, cactus and sagebrush, lone Indians against the horizon, all the Western clichés. But some of the stuff was downright spooky. There was a drawing of two men locked in a death struggle: just the faces and the straining sinews of their shoulders and necks, one white, one Indian, one shared expression of hatred. It was only a pencil sketch, but you could almost smell their sweat.

Other than the sketchpads, I found nothing that could be described as personal and nothing that connected Mariano to the Deejay or Julie Brauer or Juice.

I was sopping wet by then and decided I'd seen all there was to see. So I stepped to the door, stuck an eye to the gap, and saw that the coast was clear. After squeezing through, I turned to push the door shut and nearly jumped out of my shorts when I saw the gypsy lady standing behind it.

"You," she said.

I tried on a smile that didn't fit.

"What you want here?" she asked.

"Just came back to see Mariano."

"Still not home."

94

"Yeah, I found that out."

"You steal?"

"Oh no, no," I said, showing her my empty hands.

She tilted her head, no doubt considering me an incompetent thief. "The cops," she said.

"You called them?"

She nodded, wondering what this stupid white man was going to do next, while behind her a crowd of neighbors slinked in to join the fun.

"Thanks," I said. "Sorry to bother you. I'll be going now. Bye-bye."

I climbed the fence with about half the park's inhabitants looking on, then ran back to my truck, and fled the scene before the police arrived.

CHAPTER 17

I had time for a shower before Parkinson and Willis showed up.

When we were settled in the study, the lieutenant said, "We had a breaking-and-entering complaint we thought you might be able to help us with."

"Oh?"

"A lady at the Island Magic Trailer Court said she caught somebody leaving Mariano Santiago's unit. Her description sounded sort of familiar."

"Did it?"

"You don't have a twin, do you?"

"An only child, I'm afraid."

"Ah."

"It was me."

"Was it? That's what Willis said. 'Sounds like that fool Cochran to me,' he said. But I didn't want to believe it."

"The detective was right."

"Usually is," Parkinson agreed. "Would you mind telling us why you broke into Santiago's trailer?"

"I didn't actually break in. The door was open."

"That's something," he conceded. "Just leaves illegal entry."

"I was doing a little snooping."

"Snooping?"

"Detecting."

"I see," he said. "I wasn't aware you'd taken out an investigator's license."

"I haven't actually, but—"

"No?"

"No, but—"

"You know," he went on, "even if you *did* have a license, that still wouldn't make it legal for you to enter a residence without the consent of the owner or inhabitant. Just because they do it on TV doesn't make it right."

"Would an apology help?"

"I don't know." He glanced at Willis. "What do you think, Jake? Would it help?"

"Wouldn' hurt."

"Okay," I said. "I'm sorry. I didn't mean to get in your way on this. It's just that everybody, including *you,* seems to think I should know more than I do. And I was only trying to help."

He glanced at Willis. "Should we accept his apology?"

Willis gave me a sleepy stare. "You plannin' on doin' it again?"

"Well, no, I hadn't actually—"

He nodded. "All right then."

"Does that mean you're not charging me with illegal entry?"

Parkinson asked, "Did you say that, Jake?"

"Wudn' me."

"Then you *are* charging me?"

"He didn't say that, either. But if you were to tell us what you found, we might, and I emphasize *might,* consider letting it slide."

I handed my notes to Parkinson. He gave them a glance and handed them to Willis. "That's *it*?"

"Yeah." I was embarrassed. "Did you ask Mariano why he moved out of his trailer?"

"Uh-huh."

"What'd he say?"

"Said it was too hot because his air conditioning was on the fritz."

That sounded like a legitimate excuse to me, but . . . "Did he mention that somebody had broken in?"

He nodded. "He said that was another factor."

"Did you ask him when it happened?"

"He claimed it occurred sometime on Tuesday evening the week Hanzlik was killed."

"Coincidence?"

"Maybe."

"Did he know who did it?"

"He suggested it might have been the work of burglars."

"Was anything stolen?"

"Nothing he noticed."

"Did you search the place?"

"We took a look—with his permission, of course."

"He didn't mind?"

"Didn't seem to."

"Find anything?"

"That he's a neat housekeeper."

"Did you look at his sketchbooks?"

He nodded. "Ferocious stuff, huh?"

"Vivid."

"Would you say that the man who did those drawings was capable of violence?"

"He's too big for the Shooter, if that's what you're asking."

"Just curious."

"Who do *you* think broke into his trailer?"

"We probably made the same guess."

"The Deejay?"

"Makes sense. But we found no identifiable prints except Santiago's."

"Are you still watching him?"

"Unfortunately, we don't have enough people to keep a tail on every suspicious character in this investigation." He eyed

98

me in his mild but penetrating way. "If I asked you to stay out of this, would you?"

"Is that what you want?"

"I don't want you breaking into any more trailers."

"What if I just talk to some people?"

"Who, for example?"

"Julius Brauer?"

"I noticed you starred his name on your list of money people. You know him?"

"We've met a few times. And I thought he might be willing to see me."

"He's been up in Austin a few weeks, but he's flying back in the morning. And we're seeing him at ten."

"I could talk to him after that?"

"To pick up on what we miss?"

"I didn't mean that. I just thought he might be willing to tell me things he wouldn't tell you."

He shoved his horn-rims up his nose. "Not impossible." He stood, and Willis joined him. "I'll probably live to regret this," he said, "but as long as you make sure people are at home when you pay them a visit, I don't suppose you can do too much harm. However, I would appreciate it if you'd let us in on anything you happen to pick up."

"That's a promise."

He nodded and left, looking like he regretted his decision already.

That evening I drove up I-45 to Chili's for some soft tacos, then dropped by Buttermilk's Cue and Cushion, where Juice had once lost a thousand bucks on a scratch shot. The place was about halfway between Galveston and Houston, in a little strip center on the edge of the Baybrook Mall parking lot.

I stopped at the bar for a Corona and asked to speak to the proprietor, and the barman told me he was in the back. Buttermilk already had a game, so I claimed a table and worked on my stroke until he came over.

He was fat, over three hundred pounds, with a scraggly blond beard all over his face and very little hair on top of his head, wearing his trademark lace-fronted white shirt gapping over his belly.

Buttermilk had an old-fashioned notion that *he* at least should heed the NO GAMBLING signs that littered his walls, so we shot a few racks of straight pool just for sport. We reminisced about Juice, and I tried to pick his brain. He knew Phillie Dog and Rufus Jones but said he hadn't seen either of them in months.

When I asked if he thought Juice could have been killed over a gambling debt, he said he considered it unlikely. As he put it, "Dead men don't pay up. And Juice didn't make the size bets that get you wasted."

It was twenty-five long, monotonous miles back to Galveston, and I was having a hard time keeping my eyes open by the time Texas City appeared off to the left. Seen across the wetlands, with no large buildings to give scale, the refineries looked like a distant city on fire. The gas burnoff underlit the black cloud of polluted smoke that covered half the sky, and the hydrocarbon stink made my eyes water. But it meant I was within fifteen minutes of home.

Once across the causeway, I exited at Teichman Road and headed east on Port Industrial Boulevard. It was raised on concrete pillars over the wetlands, running without interruption for five miles, all the way down to the light at 51st Street.

I was just past the light, where the boulevard slopes down to the grain elevators, when a custom van came up quickly from behind and slowed to match my speed in the left lane. Figuring it was some brain-damaged redneck wanting to drag, I turned to flip him the bird and saw a gun pointed at me.

I slammed on the brakes so hard that the rear end started to swing around. I was afraid the pickup was going to flip over, but it didn't. The squeal of the van's tires followed mine almost immediately, but it was still skidding when I started my U-turn. I accelerated back up the elevated roadway and made a screeching left against the light onto 51st Street.

I was coming up on Broadway when I saw headlights in my rearview mirror. The stoplight ahead was just turning green, so I floored it across the intersection. Then I made a skidding turn onto Alamo Drive, narrowly missing a parked car, and fishtailed for half a block.

After that, I did fine until I started to run the stop sign on 45th Street, then had to stand on the brakes to keep from broadsiding a station wagon. I saw a frightened face, jerked the wheel hard to the right, and found myself heading straight for a tree. I stood on the brakes again and slid to a stop inches from the trunk, one wheel up on the curb.

I was pointed south now, so I headed that way and made it a few blocks before I again saw headlights coming up fast in my rearview mirror. I was flooring the accelerator when the flashing blue lights came on, and I realized I could stop running.

The cop came at me with gun drawn, and I don't think he believed me when I said, "Am I glad to see *you*."

He ordered me to climb out of the truck slowly, made me put my hands on top of the cab, and frisked me. Afterward, in spite of my protestations, he read me my rights, cuffed me, and took me down to the station.

I used my phone call to reach Parkinson and told him what had happened.

"You get a license number?" he asked.

"No."

"What about make and model?"

"Late model custom van, dark color, maybe green."

"What make?"

"Didn't notice."

"Did you get a look at the passengers?"

"All I saw was the gun."

"That doesn't help much."

"Sorry."

"And you didn't see it again after you made the U-turn?"

"Just the headlights. You know," I added, "they're about to lock me up down here. Could you ask them not to do that?"

"Is the arresting officer still there?"

"I think so."

101

"Let me talk to him."

They eventually released me under my own recognizance, but the desk sergeant insisted I'd have to face a hearing on the reckless driving charge.

I again asked for protection, but I didn't get it. So I spent another night at a motel.

The next morning, I called the Brauer number and spoke to Jeremy Parker, who was either Julie's secretary or his wife, depending on whom you asked. Whatever his position, he'd always seemed pleasant enough.

"Oh, yes, Mr. Cochran, you're Juice's friend, aren't you? We were *so* very sorry to hear of his death." He sounded like he meant it.

"Thank you. I was wondering if Mr. Brauer could spare me a few minutes this afternoon."

"May I ask what this is in reference to?"

"In reference to Juice, actually. I had a few questions I wanted to ask."

"I see," he said thoughtfully. "You're assisting the police in their investigation?"

"Oh, no," I assured him, even managing a laugh, "this has nothing to do with the police. I'm just talking to a few of Juice's friends, trying to tie up a few loose ends."

"I see." He sounded like he didn't see at all, and I couldn't blame him. "Would you hold on just a moment, Mr. Cochran?"

"All right."

He was back almost exactly sixty seconds later. "Mr. Cochran?"

"Still here."

"Would three o'clock this afternoon be convenient for you?"

"Yes, that would be fine. Thank you."

"Till then," he said. "Ta-ta."

I swear that's what he said.

In light of the debacle with Mariano, I attempted to prepare myself for this encounter. But after spending an hour trying to concoct a line of questioning, I gave it up as a lost cause. My only hope was to keep Julie talking long enough to detect something in his manner or trap him in a lie or uncover some connection, while trusting in my appearance of incompetence to keep him off guard. Incompetence, I hoped, would look like innocence.

CHAPTER 18

Julius Brauer Junior was the great-grandson of Otto Brauer, who had descended on the island after the Civil War and had made his fortune in cotton and foreclosure, and he was the grandson of Gunther Brauer, who had diversified into newspapers, hotels, banking, and insurance. Julie had a father and a mother too, of course, but Julius Senior had died when the boy was a baby, and Victoria Hammersmith Brauer had preferred to spend her time gallivanting around Europe, leaving others to raise her son.

By the early 1950s Julie had acquired a reputation as Galveston's kinkiest playboy. For ten years, he almost never left his island compound, but hundreds attended his riotous parties and left with tales of his vast pink bedroom crowded with stuffed animals, of the slide he'd had constructed from his bedroom window to the pool, and of his platoon-strength beachboy harem.

In '61, Julie abruptly emerged from his "seclusion stage" and set off on a fast lap around the world. As though the tour activated some latent money-making instinct, he entered his "tycoon stage" shortly after his return.

He bought property in Houston, then formed a construction company with a local builder, and used his property for collateral on loans to fund the building of condominiums. The company was a big success until the recession of '74 wrecked the construction industry. Then the banks called his loans due, and Julie learned a lesson: that it was better to be a lender than a borrower.

In '76, he sold off his real estate and bought a controlling interest in a respected east Texas savings and loan. He put a few cronies on the loan committee, purchased the loyalties of several directors and officers, then began steering the firm away from household mortgages into the high-risk world of commercial real estate. The Boom was on. Capital was scarce. Interest rates were high. And Julie was in the catbird seat.

He rode the crest for six years and appeared to weather the Bust of '82 without a scratch. By '84, with branches all over the state, his S&L's assets were approaching one and a half *billion* dollars.

Then came the Fall.

The Bust, in a delayed reaction, took its toll with a vengeance, as one borrower after another defaulted on loans. In late spring, the feds declared the S&L insolvent. Then they moved in and began to uncover Julie's little secrets.

He'd extorted millions in bribes and kickbacks from borrowers, while using company funds to buy himself everything from a private jet to a fleet of Mercedes. And on top of being greedy, he was stupid. Toward the end, he'd lost all control, floating loans without collateral and, in two cases, loaning money to businesses that existed only on letterheads.

He delayed legal proceedings for a year by filing Chapter 11; then indictments started coming down, and he went into hiding. He avoided state and federal authorities until last summer, when his Auntie Caroline died, and Julie suddenly forgot he was a wanted man. He emerged from his lair to attend her funeral and

105

to hear the reading of the will, in which he expected to figure prominently.

As he left the church that day, a U.S. marshal walked up, shook his hand, offered condolences, and handed him a summons. As if that wasn't enough, an even more crushing blow came when Caroline's will was read, and Julie learned that his beloved auntie had cut him out of her estate. She'd been his lone defender all those years, but this scandal had been too much even for her.

His bio made him sound like another of those colorful Texans who have made the state so popular with film and TV producers. And I'm sure that was the way Julie saw himself: as a great Texas original, an inspired combination of J. R. Ewing and Boy George. But the reality was more farcical than tragic, more repulsive than intriguing. To me, he was a moist slug of a man, utterly lacking in charisma.

While awaiting his various trials, he was under unofficial house arrest at his mother's walled mansion on Broadway: a two-story, red-tile roofed, slightly crumbling Mediterranean villa, with two great live oaks towering over the wall.

As I pulled up to the gate, a voice squawked out of a black iron box on a black iron pole: "Identify yourself."

"Bill Cochran, here to see Mr. Brauer."

After a brief delay, the gate swung inward, and the voice said, "Drive on up to the house, Mr. Cochran."

At least he didn't sign off with "Ta-ta."

The short drive ended under a portico, and Jeremy Parker came out to greet me. He was an ex-dancer-choreographer in his late thirties, looking fit and trim in his summer-weight blazer and slacks. "You can leave your car here, Mr. Cochran."

He led me through double oaken doors, down a cool, parquet-floored hallway, and through another set of double doors into a study. It was an elegant room, filled with light from tall windows overlooking a garden.

"Can I get you something?" Jeremy asked. "A drink, coffee?"

"No, thanks."

106

"Then make yourself comfortable. Mr. Brauer will be down in a moment."

As he turned to the door, Julie appeared.

He moved into the room with the measured tread of an exiled monarch. "Hello, Bull," he said with gracious condescension. "So sorry to hear about Juice. A good man and a genuine loss." He extended a damp hand, and I could see no graceful way to refuse it.

"Thank you," I said.

Taking my hand in both of his, he said, "Jerry, make us a couple of banana daiquiris." Jerry moved to obey before I could decline, and Julie assured me, "You'll love it. Juice did. We make them with just a wicked little dash of anisette."

He released my hand, then took my arm and steered me toward the windows. "Surely the police must have some leads on his killer by now?"

"None they've told me about."

His face was soft and doughy, with no character lines even in his fifties. Though I had met him half a dozen times, I could never remember what he looked like from one time to the next. It was a face always in the process of becoming, a perfect setting for his mistrustful eyes.

He offered me one of two uncomfortable gilt-and-tapestry armchairs overlooking the garden, then settled into the other and crossed his legs. He sat with elbows propped on the chair arms, hands raised like a surgeon waiting to be gloved. "Jeremy said you were assisting the police in their investigation."

"He must have misunderstood," I said. "I'm doing this strictly on my own. I sort of lost touch with Juice toward the end, and I was hoping that talking with his friends might help me fill in the gaps."

It sounded weak even to me, and I couldn't tell if he bought it. He gazed out the window, watching water splash and dazzle in the fountain. "I should tell you that my lawyers opposed my seeing you. And they adamantly insisted I answer no questions that might have bearing on any legal proceedings in which I am currently involved."

107

"It's only Juice I want to talk about."

His hands flapped, straining to escape his wrists like tethered sparrows. "His dying like that, it . . . makes one aware of one's mortality, doesn't it?"

"That it does."

He told me sincerely, "Nobody's safe."

"Nobody?"

Leaning in, he whispered, "I've been a victim myself, you know. They haven't killed me yet. Their methods have been more subtle and insidious. But, if I resist them long enough . . ." He shrugged expressively.

I nodded as though I knew what he was talking about. "Do you think these same . . . forces had anything to do with Juice's death?"

"I wouldn't be surprised."

"Who?"

"No names," he quietly insisted, hands lifted in gracious refusal. "I'm not prepared to name names at this time. That must be reserved as my last line of defense."

"Uh," I said, "when was the last time you saw Juice?"

His hands were suddenly still. "The police asked me the same question."

"Did they?"

He eyed me suspiciously for a moment, then once again glanced out the window. "I told them I saw him about two weeks before he was killed. He did me a favor by picking up some books I'd sent to Houston to be bound."

It sounded remotely plausible, and it was something the police could easily verify. "You got to know Juice on a trip to the Yucatan, right?"

"That's right." He smiled, then came to his feet and waddled toward a wall of display cases. "Almost nine years ago, back in 'seventy-nine, I hired him as a bodyguard for my Central American trip."

I joined him as he unlocked the door to one of the cases. It contained a mask of carved stone featuring a wide-eyed, open-mouthed face surrounded by a corona of sunbeams and more complex symbolism.

"Looks ancient."

"Twelfth century," he said avariciously. "The period has been verified, but the experts can't agree whether it's Mayan or Aztec. There's some intermixing of cultures indicated."

"It's exquisite," I said.

"Isn't it?" he agreed, flashing his miser's grin. "An old man in Guatemala City offered to sell it to me for a thousand dollars, but some local bureaucrats got wind of the sale and blocked it. Juice told me if I really wanted the mask he'd get it for me. I had my doubts about that, but I gave him five thousand dollars to try. A week later, I received a note from him in Mérida, telling me not to worry and saying I'd find my mask waiting for me when I got home. To be honest, I still didn't believe him, but Juice was as good as his word." He shook his head and chuckled to himself. "I always liked him for that."

He was relocking the cabinet when Jeremy appeared with our banana daiquiris.

Julie watched me take a sip. "Well?"

I was pleasantly surprised. "It's delicious." The 'wicked little dash of anisette' gave it a kick.

As Jeremy withdrew, we strolled back to the windows.

"Did you ever loan Juice money?" I asked.

"Not to my recollection," he said, as we took our seats. "He occasionally ran errands for me, and I'd give him something for his trouble."

"Something?"

He shrugged, one hand winging toward the garden. "Twenty dollars, fifty, sometimes more. To be honest, Bull," he said with a giggle, "I've always been careless with money."

I didn't say "No kidding." I asked, "Did he ever say anything to you about being in trouble?"

"I don't think so. Juice never seemed to have a care in the world."

"And you say the last time you spoke to him was two weeks before the killing?"

He nodded thoughtfully. "That was the last time I *saw* him, but I believe I actually spoke to him on the Monday before he died."

"Spoke to him?"

"That's right. He was supposed to come over but called to say he couldn't make it."

"Why not?"

"Had to go somewhere, as I recall."

"You don't happen to remember *where*?"

He gave it some thought, hands preening restlessly under his chin. "It seems to me he may have mentioned Port Bolivar."

I was considering that tidbit when Jeremy breezed in to announce that Mr. Brauer's doctor had arrived for his checkup. Julie gave me another moist handshake and said, "Good talking to you, Bull." Then Jerry graciously but firmly ushered me out of the house.

CHAPTER 19

On Wednesday, Gareth took me to lunch at Jojo's on Seawall. After we'd ordered, he gave me the doctor's once-over and said, "You don't look so good."

"Thanks."

"Haven't been sleeping?"

"Not so you'd notice."

"Is it Juice?"

"What else?"

"I'm surprised the police haven't solved this thing."

"They're not even close, as far as I can tell. In fact, they've made so little progress I actually started doing a little snooping on my own."

He cocked an amused brow. "Trying out your Philip Marlowe?"

"Closer to Inspector Clouseau, I'm afraid."

He chuckled. "Is that modesty?"

"No, honesty. I don't think I'm cut out for this business."

"Harder than it looks?"

"Much—especially a tail job."

"I beg your pardon?"

"Vehicular shadowing."

"Ah, of course."

"And then there're the all-important interviews. You know, the ones in which vital clues are revealed that lead to the solution of the crime."

"*Those* interviews."

"Right."

"No vital clues?"

"None that I can see. So far, I've talked to Mariano Santiago and Julie Brauer."

"Now, there's an odd couple."

"You know Mariano?"

"Don't know him, but I've seen him at the warehouse." He grinned. "Juice called him Crazy Horse."

Juice had nicknames for everybody. He stuck me with "Bull" and called Gareth "Dylan," after Dylan Thomas, another Welshman.

"Mariano saw right through me. I was just getting warmed up when he flatly informed me that he'd had nothin' to do with killin' Juice."

Gareth laughed. "Then you learned *something*."

"If he's telling the truth."

The waitress brought our onion soup, and we dug in, penetrating the cheese crusts and blowing on steaming spoonfuls.

"And Julie?" he asked.

"At least he talked."

"That must've been a treat."

"He's playing exiled royalty these days, so graciousness was the keynote."

"And what'd he have to say?"

I gave him a quick rundown.

"Not much substance," he decided. "So, what's your hypothesis?"

"About what?"

"Juice's murder. Who done it?"

"Haven't the foggiest."

112

"Not even a theory?"

"Just pieces, and they don't hang together so well. Julie said Juice mentioned having to go to Port Bolivar on the Monday before he died, and Lieutenant Parkinson seemed to think there might be something in that."

"Why go to Port Bolivar?"

"Maybe to pick up the suitcases I told you about."

"Drugs?"

"That was my first assumption, but now I'm thinking that maybe Julie and Juice were smuggling pre-Columbian artifacts."

"Why would Julie bring it up if he was involved?"

"Told you it wasn't a great theory."

As he bent over his soup, I saw behind him a man looking at me through the window. Not just looking in, looking at *me*. He was dark, lean, and handsome, not very tall. When he caught my eye, he smiled, then turned and glided down the sidewalk.

I was on my feet before he took his second step.

"What is it?" Gareth asked.

"The Shooter!" I called back as I headed for the door. "He's here!" I ran over a busboy, sent his dishes flying and ran on, leaving a trail of curses in my wake. I scattered a party entering the restaurant then slammed through the doors and was outside ten seconds after I'd recognized him. But the sidewalk was empty, and I saw nobody running away, heard no squealing tires.

Then it hit me that I shouldn't be standing there, that chasing a killer into the open was dumb and that making myself an easy target was just plain stupid.

So I hurried back inside, meeting Gareth on his way out.

"The manager's calling the police," he said.

"Thanks." Everybody was staring at me, but I did my best to ignore them.

"You sure it was him?" Gareth asked.

"Positive."

"An audacious bastard."

"As audacious as they come."

I told the two patrolmen what I'd seen, and they took me down to the station to look at some pictures.

Parkinson was there.

"It was him," I insisted. "That gliding step was unmistakable."

"Supposing it *was* him, why would he be playing with you like this?"

"I assume it's the Deejay's way of letting me know he still wants his suitcases."

"Maybe," he conceded.

I spent some time looking through mug shots and more of it working with an Identikit and a sketch artist.

Afterward, Parkinson examined the sketch. "What do you think?"

"The features are right," I said, "but it makes him look too much like a desperado. It misses his elegance."

"You want to try again?"

"Doubt it would help. She did her best. I just couldn't make her see the Shooter the way *I* saw him."

"Then we'll have to go with it."

"Does this mean you're going to give me some protection?"

"Can't. We still don't have enough cops."

"There's a killer on the loose, you know."

"The captain isn't convinced."

"What'll it take to convince him?"

"Your being shot at might help."

"What if I'm killed?"

"That would probably do it." When I didn't crack a smile, he said, "Why don't you spend the night at the Tremont House? The house dick's an ex-cop, and I'll ask him to keep an eye on you."

It didn't take much thought. "Okay."

"C'mon. I'll drive you."

On our way out of the building, he stopped to pick up Juice's scrapbook.

"Any help?" I asked.

"Not so far. But we'd appreciate it if you'd take a look and see if you notice anything we missed."

"Like what?"

"If I knew that—"

"I know," I said. "You wouldn't need my help?"

"Right."

The Tremont House was in the Strand Historic District, covering nearly half a square block on Mechanic Street. It occupied a nineteenth-century office building that had been lovingly converted into the most elegant hotel in town.

I splurged, putting a two-room suite and dinner from room service on my Visa card. After dinner, I lugged Juice's scrapbook to a desk in the living room. I wasn't in the mood for reminiscing, but I figured the sooner this thing was solved, the sooner I could sleep nights.

MEMORIES was stenciled across the front in peeling gold capitals. The first thirty or so pages featured Juice's relatives: browning black-and-white photos of his grandparents—skinny folks with unsmiling faces posed against dusty clapboard shacks—and parents—more black-and-white shots, gradually shifting into color, illustrating their ascension from poverty into comfortable middle class. Juice was introduced as a pudgy infant and followed through fat childhood into baseball. Little League. High school. Junior college. Semipro. Then the Big Break.

The page marking the event contained a photocopy of the contract he'd signed with the Red Sox organization. I knew the document well—I had one just like it. His was framed in gold crepe paper that had faded to pale straw.

The next page featured an 8 × 10 glossy of Juice in his gear, looking like the classic catcher: thick-necked, broad-shouldered, long-waisted, five-eleven, and tipping the scales at 190. Since retirement, he'd gained sixty pounds and looked more like the classic Southern sheriff.

This was followed by page after page of team pictures and shots of Juice: behind the plate, loping around the bases, swinging a bat. In one, he and a taller kid were standing in uniform,

115

both grinning so widely they were showing their gums. I didn't remember either of us ever looking that young. It was labeled "April 1973," our first month in the minors.

The baseball photos went on for three quarters of the scrapbook, interspersed with newspaper and magazine clippings, many of them about me. Juice didn't get much press, so he'd collected mine. Stories I didn't remember reading, interviews I didn't recall giving. They made me sound like hot stuff, a name for the future and all that. Of course, I'd thought so, too, at the time.

The last dozen or so pages in this section were devoted to the Domingo Sanchez killing. Photos, editorials, coverage of the grand jury, and so on. Shots I hadn't seen in years. One particular series of five photos snipped from a sports magazine showed the killing in graphic step-by-step detail.

The first shot caught Domingo with eyes widening at the sight of the ball coming in. In the second, he was spinning down and away, throwing up his hands and accidentally knocking his batting helmet half off his head. The third froze him at the instant the ball struck him behind the ear, in an area formerly covered by his helmet. The fourth showed him on the way down. And the fifth had him on the ground, one hand folded awkwardly under his chin, an elbow sticking uselessly into the air.

It had taken me years to get that series of pictures out of my mind, and seeing them again took my breath away.

116

CHAPTER 20

Thursday was a slow day at the warehouse, and we started a general clean-up after lunch. About 3:00, Mariano asked if he could get off to run some errands.

As he pulled out of the lot, I sprinted for my pickup. I kept him in sight all the way down Broadway, past the turnoff to his rented room and the one to the trailer park, all the way down to 61st Street, where he took the underpass south toward the seawall.

After coming off the causeway over Offatts Bayou, I pulled into the left lane to pass a slow-moving car, and Mariano made a quick right onto Stewart Road.

I couldn't get over to make the turn, but I claimed the right lane just beyond the light and squealed across a shopping center parking lot back to Stewart Road. It ran straight for about two hundred yards, then curved south. I took the curve, still seeing no sign of Mariano's jeep, and hugged a station wagon's tailgate, blowing my horn until it pulled over. Then I floored the accelerator as the road veered back to the right. I was doing seventy by the time it straightened out heading west and was passing ninety as Sea-Arama appeared off to my left.

I finally caught sight of Mariano about a hundred yards ahead and eased off a bit, keeping him there for the next six miles.

He caught me off guard when he made the right onto Twelve Mile Road. I'd let him get too far ahead, and, by the time I made the turn, the road was empty ahead. The cultured green contours of Galveston Country Club and Golf Course rolled away to the left, and scrubby grassland stretched off to the right, with herds of horses grazing in rainwater up to their fetlocks. Beyond the horses, on a road that cut across the field, I caught a glimpse of Mariano's jeep.

The unnamed road snaked its way through marshy fields, past clumps of stables, a decaying show ring, and a few isolated houses. Somebody had started repairing the road, but they'd run out of gravel after the first quarter mile. Beyond that, avoiding the deepest ruts took most of my concentration, and I was lucky to catch a glimpse of the jeep as I jolted past. It was parked behind a huge oleander bush in the driveway of a vacant house.

I didn't see Mariano at first, but I finally located him off to the left, hiking through an overgrown field toward a line of trees marking the bank of the bayou.

I kept him in sight as I pulled about fifty feet farther down the road and parked on a sandy verge. Then I grabbed my binoculars out of the glove compartment and climbed into the bed for elevation.

I got the glasses focused in time to see Mariano step between two trees, drop down a bank, and disappear. I itched to follow him and see what he was up to, but I didn't want him to spot me. So I stayed where I was.

Five minutes passed, then ten, and I was starting to think he'd given me the slip when he suddenly reappeared, lugging two black garbage bags. Judging from his effort, they were fairly heavy.

I pulled farther down the road and concealed the pickup behind a garage-size clump of brambles. Then I waited for Mariano to pull out and followed him back to Stewart Road.

If it *was* the suitcases, did that mean Mariano was involved in killing Juice? I didn't want to believe it. But there was worse to come.

It happened on a familiar weed-lined straightaway between Ten and Nine Mile Roads. The jeep slowed, brakelights flashing, and turned north onto another narrow lane. I knew the road. It led to several ranches, the first of which belonged to Gareth.

I coasted to a stop and sat there blocking Stewart until a squeal of tires and a blaring horn prodded me into following Mariano. I pulled down the road far enough to get a clear view of the house sitting on top of a slight, man-made rise, then grabbed the glasses and spotted Mariano heading his jeep up the driveway. Shifting the glasses to the house, I saw that both cars were gone.

Mariano parked at the house, took out the garbage bags and disappeared. When he returned a few minutes later without the bags, I backed out onto Stewart.

Mariano being involved in this was bad enough. But Gareth? I couldn't believe he'd have anything to do with killing Juice. He was Juice's friend and mine. Now that Juice was dead, he was the best friend I had.

Maybe it *wasn't* the suitcases. That was possible, something worth considering, but I didn't believe it.

Gareth had said he didn't know Mariano. And the fact that a man entered your property didn't necessarily mean you knew that man. But I didn't believe that either.

"So you didn't actually see the suitcases," Parkinson said when I called.

"No."

"And Doctor Llewellyn wasn't home."

"Didn't look like it. Neither of the cars was there."

"And you don't know where Santiago went from the ranch?"

"No, I left in a hurry."

"All right," he said. "You did good work. This may actually mean something. But I want you to let us handle it from here on. Understand?"

"Right."

"Does that mean yes?"

"Yes."

"Hmmm." He sounded like he had his doubts.

Concerned about my credit card balance, I risked going home again that night, and Molly came by around 6:30 to pick up a few more details. I talked her into staying for dinner, but I wasn't the best of company.

They hadn't found Mariano yet, but his room and trailer were being watched. Gareth and Sybil had reportedly driven up to see a play at the Alley Theater in Houston. According to Mrs. Livingston, their housekeeper, they wouldn't be returning until tomorrow. And the police would wait until they got back before searching their property.

"By the way," Molly told me, "we found a witness who confirmed seeing Harvey take the ferry to Port Bolivar the Monday before he died."

"Do you know where he went?"

"Not yet."

"Think it means anything?"

"Every little bit helps." She examined me. "Are you all right?"

I shrugged. "This thing with Gareth wasn't what I had in mind."

"I know."

"It makes me feel sort of guilty."

"You didn't do anything wrong."

"I know it doesn't make any sense. But if *you'd* found something to implicate him, that would be one thing. It's your job. With me, it seems like . . . prying."

"Don't jump the gun on this," she said. "Even if we find the suitcases there, that doesn't necessarily mean he *did* anything."

"What're the odds?"

120

"I wouldn't lay a bet either way."

Walking her out to her car, I asked, "What about our picnic at the beach house on Saturday?"

"I arranged to get off, if you still want me to come?"

"What do you think?"

She flashed a grin. "That I'll be seeing you on Saturday?"

"Smart girl."

CHAPTER 21

The bedside clock said 2:23 A.M. Something had awakened me. I didn't know what.

When a shadow moved at the foot of the bed, I tried to sit up. But a larger shadow slammed me back down and pressed something cold to my forehead.

"That's a gun," the first shadow said. "Don't give him an excuse to use it." There was a touch of Ricardo Montalban in his accent, a matter of rhythms more than pronunciation.

"What do you want?"

"Why? Does my being here make you nervous?"

Sounding as tough as my position allowed, I said, "Should it?"

"Oh, yes." His teeth gleamed in the light from the window. "In your place, *I* would be nervous."

I worked up enough spit to separate my lips. "What are you going to do?"

The grin widened. "It's not a matter of *what,* my friend, only *when.*"

"How about *why?*"

That provoked a sophisticated little jet-set chuckle. "I just wanted you to know I'm still here."

"That's all you came for?"

"Isn't it enough?"

It was, but I didn't say so.

"You must be thirsty." He told his partner, "Why don't you give Mr. Cochran a drink?"

When I pulled away from the glass, the Shooter assured me, "It's not poisoned. That wouldn't be very sporting. It's merely something to help you sleep." Another dry chuckle. "I doubt you'll get much rest without it."

He had a point, but I still resisted.

"You can drink," he said quietly, "or you can die."

The stuff tasted foul, orange juice mixed with something bitter, but I managed to choke it down.

The two stood and waited for me to get sleepy. It didn't take long. When my eyes wanted to close, I let them. But I pried them open when I heard movement and caught a last glimpse of the Shooter gliding through the doorway. I think I tried to reach the phone.

I slept through the alarm and didn't wake until ten. Doctor Riggins established with a blood test that I'd been knocked out by a state-of-the-art soporific called Halcyon. He suggested I try something milder the next time or a smaller dosage.

As a positive effect, the police were finally convinced I might actually be in danger, and they grudgingly restored my twenty-four-hour surveillance.

Mariano hadn't showed up for work that morning, and Parkinson didn't know where he was. But a man on Bayou Vista had spotted somebody fitting Mariano's description hanging around his car last night. The car had turned up in Texas City this morning, and another vehicle had been stolen nearby. Gareth and Sybil were on their way back from Houston, and Parkinson was heading out to their place to search for the garbage bags.

I manned the office phones, feeling groggy but restless and tired of sitting around. I complained for the umpteenth time about the busted air conditioner. Only, this time, Tony had a solution.

"Probably just needs Freon," he said.

"That's *all*?"

"Could be."

I couldn't believe it. "Do you know how long that thing's been out?"

"Coupla weeks?"

"You've been suffering in here with me. Why didn't you say something?"

He shrugged. "You told me you were taking care of it."

"I tried, but they put me on a waiting list."

"You want me to go out and get some Freon?"

"Would you?"

"Sure."

He brought back a canister of Freon, which did the trick with the AC, and some tuna salad sandwiches and chips for lunch.

When we sat down to eat, he said, "Can I ask you somethin'?"

"Sure."

"What's goin' on?"

"What do you mean?"

"Where's Mariano?"

"He's gone."

"Left town?"

"Apparently."

He took a bite and chewed, putting it together. "So they think he had something to do with killin' Juice?"

"Well, it doesn't look good, his disappearing like this."

He scratched his head, then shook it. "You never know with people, do you?"

"Nope."

"I mean you work with a guy six years, and you figure you know him. And what you *don't* know, you make up . . . sorta fill in the blanks, you know?"

"Yeah."

"He never had much to say, but I figured he had his reasons—some secret in his past, you know. Something bad, maybe, but not *too* bad. He was a good worker, always pulled his weight, never made any trouble. Even had a second job."

"He *did?*"

"Yeah."

"Doing what?"

"Driving for Island Antiques."

That was news to me.

"I figured you knew about it."

I shook my head. "Did he tell you?"

"No. I saw him in their van one day."

"When?"

"Coupla months ago."

"Hunh."

"It's funny," he said, shaking his head. "I imagined that he was workin' hard and savin' his money to put somebody through college. You know, a younger brother or sister, somebody like that."

"You never know," I said, distracted, having just remembered that we had a delivery for Island Antiques going out this afternoon. I didn't usually believe in signs, but in my drug-befogged state, I took it as an omen that a perfect excuse for visiting Island Antiques should present itself just when I needed one.

I should have told Parkinson immediately, of course, but I knew he'd insist that I stay away from Island Antiques, and I wanted to check the place out. I had finally managed to ferret out a possibly significant clue, and I wasn't about to give it up until I knew what I had.

That afternoon, I left Tony to man the phones and loaded the deliveries into my pickup. At 3:45, after doing a bit of socializing at each stop, I eased up to the back of Island Antiques, and the patrol car parked behind me.

I'd called ahead, and there was a boy waiting for me in the storeroom, with the power door raised. I passed him two captain's chairs wrapped in bubble plastic, then hollered at the patrolmen, telling them I'd be a few minutes.

125

As I climbed in, I saw a door being pulled shut to my right. It led into a room in the corner, a sheetrocked addition that was built out from the concrete-block walls, a little bigger than a walk-in closet. I'd have liked a peek inside.

When the boy reached for the invoice, I told him, "I need your boss to sign this."

"Since when?"

"New company policy," I lied.

"Yeah?"

"Yep."

He jerked a thumb. "He's up front."

"Mind if I look around first?"

He thought it strange. "Back here?"

"Just want to see what you got. I'm thinking of furnishing my house with antiques."

He shrugged. "Guess it's okay."

The room was jammed with furniture, tables and chairs stacked two and three high, leaving scant room for a small workshop area. I picked my way through the stacks, pretending to find it all intriguing, though the only area of interest was the room in the corner. Since the door was still closed, I decided to try it again on my way out.

The door at the front of the storeroom opened into the shop behind the counter, where the proprietor was showing a man a clock.

I said, "I need somebody to sign this."

He told his customer, "Hang on," and glanced at the invoice. "We expected this Tuesday. Just hope you haven't cost me a sale."

"Wouldn't want that," I said, "but the holdup was at the other end."

He was skeptical but pulled out a pen.

And his customer said, "I'll look around."

I'd only heard the voice once, almost two weeks before, but that supercilious tone was unmistakable.

I must have made a sound because he was suddenly looking at me. And he knew me, too. "Grab him!" the Deejay barked.

126

Fortunately, the owner didn't know what he was talking about. As he turned to the Deejay, I went for the door.

It opened as I reached for the knob, and a big man in a dark suit and mirrored sunglasses stuck his head in to say something.

I kicked the door shut in his face as the Deejay snapped, "Get him!" And I was rolling over the counter when the door crashed open behind me.

The Deejay reached for me but missed. I hurdled a tufted ottoman and knocked over a Dutch highboy. Then, to the accompaniment of shattering china, I skidded around an Early American dry sink and started for the door.

It opened with a tinkling of bells, and another large man stepped inside. I thought help had arrived until I registered the dark suit and mirrored sunglasses and figured that was too much of a coincidence.

As I skidded to a halt, something slammed into my shoulder, and my left arm went numb. I lashed out with my right but missed, and my momentum spun me around. I caught a glimpse of one dark suit with an arm held high just as the other clubbed me from behind.

CHAPTER 22

Consciousness returned in stages, pain first. My head felt cracked open. The first heartbeat sent me back into unconsciousness, and the first time I tried to open my eyes it had the same effect. On the next try, I made out some blurry shapes, but it required several more attempts to bring a clear image into focus.

What I saw wasn't reassuring.

I was folded into the back of a custom van, hands cuffed behind me, shoulder throbbing. It was the same van, I assumed, from which somebody had pointed a gun at me on Monday. Two of my captors sat on the rear bench seat, one of the dark suits to the Deejay's right. And I assumed the other was driving. Their patron was slender and resplendent in a pearl-gray summer three-piece. There was nothing special about his face except for its unnatural paleness and the eyes—icy gray, almost transparent.

They focused on me. "He's awake. Blindfold him."

"With what?" the clone asked.

"Use your tie."

128

He reluctantly stripped off his cravat and bent to tie it around my head.

"Make it tight," the boss ordered.

A few minutes later, the van veered from smooth pavement onto gravel. It stopped, and somebody moved past me to open the side door, letting in the heat. Two pairs of hands pulled me out of the van, took me by the legs and shoulders, and crunched across a stretch of gravel. Sunlight filtered dimly through the silk but cut off as I was carried down some steps into a dark room smelling of dampness and fresh paint. They lowered me onto cool concrete, then walked away, and the door was closed.

I lay still for a moment, listening, and decided I was alone. I was lying on my bad arm, so I rolled over and collided with the wall. I tried to work off the blindfold against it, but I couldn't get enough traction. Both wall and floor were too smooth. I wriggled along the wall looking for a more abrasive surface, but what I found was a puddle.

I sniffed it and touched my tongue to it. Water, a bit oily, but not bad considering the source. After quenching my thirst, I squirmed back a couple of feet and considered my situation.

On the plus side, I was alive. It was a big plus but readily subject to change. I knew the Deejay wanted his suitcases, and I knew where to find them, or at least thought I knew. But if they were inside those garbage bags, they could already be in the hands of the police. And if I told the Deejay that, he might decide he had no reason to keep me alive. He'd already ordered one killing, and I'd seen his face.

I could send the Deejay to Gareth's ranch and hope the police caught him. That sounded like a good idea until I gave it some thought. What if he dispatched one of his boys to check it out, and he didn't come back? Then the Deejay would know I'd tried to trick him. Besides, nobody was dumb enough to go strolling into a place swarming with police. And if the cops were gone and Gareth and Sybil were home alone, I couldn't see myself leading three armed men into their living room.

So what could I do?

I could tell him the suitcases were at my house, but I couldn't be sure the police would be watching it. The same applied to the warehouse. They had searched it thoroughly, establishing that the suitcases weren't hidden there, and they would be putting every available officer on the hunt for me. There was always Anna Mae's house to consider. The Deejay might believe Juice had hidden the suitcases there, but once again I couldn't be sure the cops would be watching it. And I couldn't expose Anna Mae to that kind of danger any more than I could Gareth and Sybil.

I was still trying to decide on a story when the door opened, and I got a faint impression of light.

The Deejay said, "Find the switch."

I heard a soft click, then the door was closed, and still fainter light filtered through the blindfold. Footsteps approached, and I yelped in pain as they wrenched my shoulder jerking me off the floor. The boys shoved me into a chair and lashed me to it at chest and ankles.

Then another chair scraped across the concrete, and the Deejay said mildly, "I should have done this at the start and saved us both a lot of trouble. Where are my suitcases?"

I was winging it. "At my house."

"Where did you find them?"

"In an unused chest freezer at Anna Mae Boatman's place."

"Who's she?"

"The woman who raised Juice."

"When did you discover them?"

"Wednesday afternoon."

"What was inside?"

This was the test. "Cocaine."

When he snarled, "Hurt him!" I knew I'd flunked.

One twin held me from behind while the other worked from the front. He slapped me across the face, going forehand and backhand, playing tennis with my head. When I tried to jerk away, his hand landed on my ear, and my head rang like a gong.

He was just finding his rhythm when the Deejay told him, "Enough. I want him conscious." As the hands released me from behind, he said, "So you don't have my suitcases."

"No."

"Where have you looked?"

"Everywhere."

"Obviously not."

"I gave the police a list of all the places where Juice lived, all those I knew."

"Perhaps they were hidden some place he only visited."

"I gave them that list, too."

He scooted his chair closer. "I don't think you understand your situation. Your only hope for getting out of here alive—and it's slim at best—is that you help me find my suitcases."

"I've tried."

"No, you haven't." The angrier he got, the quieter he spoke. "You went straight to the police. We had a business agreement, an agreement entered into by me in good faith, and you broke that agreement. Now you lie to me. I must tell you that I'm becoming increasingly impatient. If I don't get what I want, I can promise you not only death but a great deal of pain beforehand. Do you understand that?"

"Yes."

"Good." The chair was pushed back.

"What do we do with him?" one of the boys asked.

"Indulge yourself. Oh, Bully Boy?"

"Yes?"

"When you awaken, I encourage you to devote all your deductive powers to the mystery of where the Juicer might have hidden my suitcases."

"I'll do that."

"Perfect." He walked away; the door opened and closed.

The boys took their former positions, one behind, one in front. The one in front began with a punch to my nose, wrecking Doctor Riggins's handiwork, and followed it with a sharp uppercut that loosened my dental work. Then he started coming at me with lefts and rights, each punch detonating inside my head. Blackness was washing in when I heard his partner say, "Leave me some." And they changed places.

This one opened by leaning in and burying his fist in my gut. But it was a choice he quickly lived to regret. Before he could get out of the way, he was struck head-on by a geyser of half-digested tuna salad and chips.

"Look at this shit!" he raged.

"Puke," his twin said.

"I know it's puke, you flamin' asshole! I'll show the sumbitch to puke on me." He leaned in close enough for me to smell his garlicky breath and went to work on my ribs, really putting his heart into it this time. When he brought a fist up from underneath, I felt something pop. And the next punch put me out of my misery.

CHAPTER 23

I was awakened by something with lots of legs crawling on my face. Screaming didn't deter its march, and shaking my head only hurt me. So I crushed the little beastie against my shoulder until it stopped squirming, then tried to find a clean spot on which to wipe off the remains.

I was still blindfolded and strapped to the chair, hands cuffed behind me. I smelled urine and recalled with embarrassment that I had peed on myself during the night. Registering fresh pressure in that area, I clamped my legs together and tried to concentrate on something else.

I wasn't sure how much time had passed, but judging from the emptiness of my stomach, I decided it had to be early Saturday morning.

When I remembered what had happened to my lunch, I had to chuckle. Chuckling hurt, but it didn't stop me. Everything hurt: head, neck, shoulders (the left one in particular), back, belly, and *rib*. The rib was the worst. It was pain like a knife, firmly embedded in the muscle, twisted by breathing. The deeper the breath, the more it hurt, so I was reduced to panting. My nose

133

was clotted shut, and my mouth was dry as ashes from sleeping with it open. I knew there was a puddle near the wall and wondered if I could reach it, but when I tried to turn the chair around, my rib convinced me I wasn't that thirsty.

Since the Deejay could show up at any moment, I started racking my brain for a place I could send him to look for the suitcases. I needed a location the police would be watching, where there would be no civilians to get in the way of any stray bullets. But to save my life (and it was at stake here), I couldn't think of a place that met both criteria.

This study period lasted so long that I eventually had to relieve the pressure on my bladder, adding to the already strong stench of urine. Hours passed, but only one idea came to mind, and it was a long shot.

"Suit of armor?"

"It's real," I said. "I've seen it since that night."

I could almost hear him frown. "Why did you suddenly happen to remember it?"

"Maybe I never had such a good reason before."

"Hmmm," he said.

"I was only there once seven years ago, and I don't even know if the house is still there. But it's the only other place I can think of."

"Could you find it again?"

"I think so." At that moment, I was just trying to avoid another beating.

He finally said, "All right," and told the boys, "Bring him."

When I asked if I could go to the toilet first, he said there wasn't time.

But one of the twins complained, "The fucker smells of piss already."

The other echoed, "Yeah, he stinks."

And the Deejay decided he could spare the time after all.

134

The boys escorted me up a double flight of stairs to a floor that smelled of sawdust, glue, and fresh paint.

When they tried to shove me into the toilet, I said, "I'm gonna need some help."

"Help?"

"Pulling down my jeans."

"What the *fuck* you talkin' about?"

"My hands are tied behind me, remember?"

"You can shit in yer pants fer all I care!"

"Yeah," said his twin.

"Okay," I agreed, "but you'll have to live with the smell."

"Aw, fuck," the first moaned. He told his buddy, "You say anything about this and I'll tear yer fuckin' head off."

My jeans were unzipped and jerked down to my thighs.

"Undies, too," I said.

"What the fuck you—"

"The smell, remember?"

"Jesus, fuckin' . . ."

I enjoyed his embarrassment, but I was pleased that the position of my hands allowed me to wipe my own ass.

We were somewhere beyond the western end of the seawall when they removed my blindfold. One of the boys was driving, the Deejay to his right. The other was in the back with me. According to my seatmate's digital watch, it was 6:23 A.M. I could see through the small circular window to my left that it was a somber morning, with sea and sky the same dingy gray. My broken rib still stabbed me at every breath, and my shoulder burned from the strain of having my hands cuffed behind me. But at least I could see where we were going.

The Deejay asked without turning, "How far out is it?"

"Pretty far, I think."

"You *think*?"

"That's how I remember it."

We drove on and on.

When the beach houses vanished at the edge of the state park, the Deejay turned and shoved his mirrored sunglasses up his nose. All three were wearing them now, constituting a fair share of the mirrored sunglass market. "This better not be a trick," he said.

"No trick."

"Why don't I believe you?"

I decided to treat that as a rhetorical question, assuming that anything I said would only make him more suspicious.

He was still staring at me when the driver said, "I don't fuckin' believe it."

I couldn't see it at first through the little window, but I caught a glimpse as we passed—my trusty, rusty suit of armor, standing steadfast at the side of the road.

I tried not to think about what would happen after the Deejay discovered that the suitcases weren't at the house. My actions were still an exercise in avoiding pain.

"Where to now?" he asked.

I considered trying to delay matters by keeping him wandering from one beach development to the next. But I didn't think the Deejay would tolerate much wandering.

"Keep going," I said. "Look for a beach access sign."

On the other hand, if I really hadn't been here in seven years, I couldn't find it too easily. So, when the beach access road intersected with the one running parallel to the shore, I suggested we try the left branch first. Since I could only see one side of the road at a time, I made the driver go slowly down the road and back. It killed a few minutes, but after that there was no choice but to try the other branch.

When the house finally appeared in my little window, I told the driver, "Hold it."

We stopped, and the Deejay turned. "Well?"

Still trying to leave myself a way out, I said, "This *looks* like it."

"But you're not sure?"

"Seven years is a long time. But this fits what I remember."

He nodded, and the driver eased the van onto the shoulder.

Hearing a voice drifting up from the beach as we climbed

out, I thought about yelling for help. But there was nobody in sight, and I was afraid to risk it.

We circled around the collapsed carport and followed the overgrown path through the waist-high weeds up to the house. When the Deejay saw the empty utility room and the broken padlock, he turned to me with a suspicious set to his mouth. Then he eyed the stairs and decided to risk one of the twins on it first. He followed, with me and the other twin bringing up the rear.

The Deejay took a quick look around the front room, wrinkling his nose at the stink of mildew, then headed for the bedrooms. He walked through both of them quickly, leaving the free twin to check the closets. In the second bedroom he sent an empty quart Blue Ribbon bottle spinning with a kick.

Back in the main room, he stared at me for a moment, eyes hidden behind his mirrored lenses. "Any other ideas?"

"It's possible this isn't the right house, or even the right development."

His mouth tightened.

"We could try some others," I suggested.

I wouldn't have been surprised if he'd pulled out a gun and shot me. Instead, he brusquely ordered one twin to check out the storage room attached to the carport and told the other to take me back to the van. He trailed us down the steps.

The lead twin loped ahead. He was ducking under the high side of the carport roof when he suddenly stopped and back-pedaled in a hurry, reaching into his jacket.

A voice shouted something from under the collapsed roof, but the twin kept backing and reaching. I heard a flat crack, and he jerked backward. As he went down, my escort released my arm, going for his weapon. And I seized the moment.

I took a step back for leverage, then brought up my boot as hard as I could, planting the toe in his scrotum. It was exquisitely satisfying and excruciatingly painful, the jolt to my rib dropping me to my knees.

Then Willis was on me, growling, "Stay down," as cops appeared everywhere. They came out from under the house, one knocking the second twin to the ground with a rifle butt. They rose out of the tall grass, exploded on three-wheelers over the dunes, scrambled over the fences. Sirens whooped, brakes screeched, and tires skidded in gravel as reserve troops arrived on the scene. They must have called out every cop in south Texas.

"How'd you know?" I asked Willis.

"I didn't know nothin'," he drawled. "Ask *her*."

"Who?"

He jutted his chin over my shoulder, and I turned to see Molly in a flak-vest, holstering her revolver as she came down the steps.

Behind her, handcuffed, and in the firm grasp of two officers, was the Deejay. He looked mussed and unhappy, blood staining his gray suit and white shirt, and he'd lost his sunglasses somewhere.

Willis helped me up. Molly tossed him the keys to my cuffs, and he got them unlocked in time for me to wave goodbye to the Deejay, who gave me a withering glare as he passed.

With Molly near, I was suddenly conscious of the urine stink that surrounded me like a fog. Hoping she wouldn't notice, I asked, "How'd you know?"

She grinned. "Do I look like the kind of girl to miss a date?"

I grinned back and seemed to lose myself in her eyes. Sea-green, they were, littered with flecks of gold, the pupils so black, so deep, they seemed to draw me in, expanding as I watched . . .

Then Molly was holding me up, and Parkinson was at my other shoulder.

"Need a stretcher?" he asked.

"Depends on how far I have to walk."

He smiled (the first I had ever personally elicited). "Not far."

"Never really expected to see you guys."

"You almost didn't," he said. "I wanted to concentrate our forces at Llewellyn's house, but Detective Flanagan insisted we put at least half of them here. And she finally convinced me she knew what she was talking about."

138

They stuffed me into the back seat with Molly to hold me up, and Willis pointed us toward town.

"What about the suitcases?" I asked.

Parkinson turned. "They were there, in the garbage bags. We found them in one of the outbuildings."

"How'd Gareth take it?"

"He didn't seem concerned at all when we served the warrant. Amused, in fact. Told us by all means to look around, take our time. He was so relaxed I started to think we might be wrong. When we found the suitcases, he was shocked, and I think it was genuine. He really didn't know they were there."

"So Mariano planted them to throw the scent off himself."

He nodded. "But I suspect Llewellyn's involved in this somehow."

"Why?"

"Why else would Santiago have picked his place to plant the suitcases?"

I didn't have an answer for that one. "Is he under arrest?"

"Doctor Llewellyn?" He shook his head. "We questioned him and asked him not to leave town for a while. But we have no evidence he committed a crime."

"I can't picture him having Juice killed."

"We still don't know about that. In fact, there's a *lot* we don't know. We have some of the perpetrators, but we're a little hazy on the charges."

"At least you have the drugs."

"Drugs?"

"In the suitcases."

Molly grinned, and Parkinson honored me with a second smile. "Okay," I said, "so what was in the suitcases?"

He adjusted his horn-rims. "A hundred and seventy-five thousand in assorted bills."

CHAPTER 24

They put a pin in my broken rib that afternoon and even made an effort to repair my nose. But it would take more than that to make it straight again.

Molly said it would give me character.

"Great," I told her. "Now I'll never get them to stop calling me Bull." She really dressed up a hospital room in her red jumpsuit, and I couldn't take my eyes off her. "How's the case coming?"

"We've picked up a few more pieces, such as the Deejay's real name—Jackson Wheeler."

That rang a bell.

"Sound familiar?"

"I've heard it somewhere."

"He hosted a syndicated radio talk show originating in Houston called 'Wheeling with Wheeler.'"

"So he *was* a deejay?"

"Close enough. As you know, Mariano Santiago drove a van for Island Antiques. He made monthly deliveries to Montrose

Antiques in Houston. And we just found out that Wheeler is a part-owner in the Houston store."

"Ah-hah."

"The two stores had an exchange agreement. If one had two brass beds, they might trade one for a four-poster or something."

"But it wasn't really antiques they were trading?"

"Not exclusively. We also found traces of cocaine in the van and in a storeroom at the Houston shop."

"Where'd they get the stuff?"

"From Doctor Llewellyn, we think. But we have yet to prove it."

When she finally got up to go, I asked, "Am I still a suspect?"

She grinned. "I suppose we can now safely eliminate you from suspicion."

"Well, when you leave a man in his bed, it's customary to part with a kiss."

"Sir!"

"Shocked?"

"A little."

"You don't look it."

She glanced at the door. "What if somebody walks in?"

"They can get their own kiss."

"I thought you were a sick man."

"Not *that* sick."

She examined me briefly, then leaned down and let her lips linger on mine for a moment.

"I could learn to enjoy that," I whispered.

"So could I," she conceded, "in time." After another glance at the door, she said, "I guess one more for the road wouldn't hurt."

Gareth phoned me Sunday morning to see how I was doing. It was a perfectly natural thing for a friend to do, of course. But

141

since neither of us wanted to be the first to bring up the subject of drugs or murder, the conversation was brief and punctuated with silences.

Anna Mae came by with a piece of lemon meringue pie and sat with me for a while. After she left, Parkinson showed up to report that Mariano was on his way back to Galveston.

"We lucked out," he said. "He was clocked in a speed trap outside Brownsville and ran his car off the road during the chase. He's being flown back now."

"Is Wheeler talking yet?"

"Yeah. We couldn't get his boys to shut up, and I guess he figured we ought to hear *his* side of the story."

"Did he order Juice's murder?"

"Claims he had nothing to do with it. Said he'd arranged to meet Hanzlik at the warehouse at twelve-thirty that Saturday morning and was approaching the gate when he saw two figures crossing the lot. He held back until they left, then sent one of his boys up close enough to see blood through the office door. After that, he claims to have ordered a retreat to your house."

"Do you believe him?"

He shrugged. "It fits the facts."

"If *he* didn't have Juice killed, who did?"

"Good question."

"You think it's Gareth, don't you?"

"He's a suspect."

"What would have been his motive?"

"Eliminating a witness to his participation in the cocaine trade?"

I shook my head. "I still don't want to believe it."

"It's just a theory."

"Did Wheeler implicate him?"

"Didn't mention him. Neither did his boys."

"Then maybe . . ."

"Yeah," he agreed. "Maybe."

I left the hospital the next morning and took a cab to the warehouse. Because I was too doped up to be useful, I left Tony in charge and had Randy give me a lift home.

142

Parkinson and Willis arrived a few minutes later. Willis doffed his straw hat, and Parkinson asked, "How're you feeling?"

"Beat to a pulp."

"Won't keep you long, but we had some information we thought you'd want to hear." Once settled in the study, he went on, "Santiago says he spotted the suitcases that Wednesday morning when you were rearranging the storage boxes."

"Yeah. He helped me do it."

"But he claims he didn't remove them until the morning after Harvey was killed."

"I was there that morning."

"Said he did it while you were at the doctor's office."

"Right. I forgot about that."

"He was planning to take the cash and head for South America."

"What stopped him?"

"Said he was afraid we'd tie him to the murder if he disappeared too soon. But when he thought we were getting close, he took out twenty-five thousand, planted the rest at Llewellyn's place, and headed for Mexico."

"What'd he say about Gareth?"

"They met on Grand Cayman in 'eighty-two. Llewellyn was ostensibly down there for a vacation, and somebody gave him Santiago's name as a go-between."

"Who?"

"Santiago won't say, and Llewellyn claims not to know what we're talking about. Anyway, he allegedly hired Santiago to make the buy and to arrange to have the stuff smuggled into the country. After using him again a few months later, Llewellyn decided to take him on full time. Wheeler didn't know about Llewellyn because Santiago handled all personal contact. He was paid well for it, too. Started out at five thousand a month, got a raise to seventy-five hundred, and says he pulled down over a hundred thousand last year. The shipments were small, as these things go, but if what Santiago says is true, Llewellyn must have cleared between three and four million during the six years."

"Where'd he stash it?"

"Don't know yet. But we've learned he made at least one trip to Geneva each of the last six years."

"Ah."

"According to Santiago, they started demanding money in advance about a year ago, after Wheeler was slow to come up with the cash on one occasion. The coke would be smuggled in, and Santiago would stash it at Island Antiques. Then he would notify Wheeler that a shipment could be delivered, and Wheeler would drop the suitcases at a prearranged spot."

"Such as Port Bolivar."

"Yeah. Hanzlik would pick up the cash and take it to Llewellyn, who would then notify Santiago to make the delivery."

"Why didn't Wheeler and his boys go after Mariano?"

"They *did,* on Tuesday night, but he chased them away from his trailer with a shotgun. They followed him from work on Wednesday, but he lost them and spent the night on Llewellyn's boat. On Thursday, he left his jeep at the warehouse, climbed over the back fence, and checked into a hotel. Said he hid out in various places for the next four days before taking the room off Forty-second, but he didn't see the Deejay again until last Wednesday."

"The night before he went after the suitcases."

"Right."

"I'm amazed he stuck around after Juice was murdered. Wasn't he afraid he was next on the list?"

"I wondered about that, too. But I think he did it for personal reasons."

"Meaning what?"

"He's an icy character, this Santiago. The only time I saw any sign of a thaw was when he mentioned Wheeler's name. He really hates the man, and I think he hung around because he got a kick from outsmarting him."

I shook my head. "It still doesn't add up."

"What doesn't?"

"Juice's murder. If he was Wheeler's only hope for recovering the money, why would Wheeler have him killed? And I'm still not ready to believe that Gareth would do it."

"No rush," he said. "We're not finished yet."

"Are you still watching this house?"

"No, the surveillance was pulled off after we booked Wheeler."

"What about the Shooter?"

"He's one of the reasons we came by. We sent your sketch and description to the FBI, and they came up with a possible ID." He slipped two 8 × 10s out of a manila envelope. "They're blowups of telephoto shots and not very clear."

The first was a full-length picture of a young man walking down a flight of steps, dressed in a white double-breasted suit and a white flat-brimmed hat. The face was dark and turned to the side, revealing a handsome profile cut off just above the left eyebrow by his hat brim. The other shot was a blowup of the first. It was awfully grainy but showed the classic profile in greater detail: square jaw, chiseled chin, Roman nose, high cheekbone.

"You don't have one full face?"

"That's all they sent us."

I took another look. "Lousy pictures," I said. "All I can tell you is this *could* be the man I saw outside Jojo's."

He nodded and slid the photos back into their envelope. "According to the feds, he may or may not be Cuban. He's in his early twenties, believed to be fluent in several languages, including English, and he's supposed to be a real pro. They say he works fast and gets out of the country even faster. So, for what it's worth, they suggest he was probably back in Havana twelve hours after he hit Hanzlik."

"How do they explain all the sightings?"

"They question the accuracy of your sightings, and they express surprise at finding him dabbling in the commercial market, as he allegedly specializes in political hits. They conclude by suggesting that perhaps this wasn't the man you saw."

"That's great. They say this is the man, then they explain why it can't be him."

145

"Confusing, isn't it?"

"Well, if it's *not* him, that means he could still be around, right?"

"It's possible. But professional hit people don't work for nothing, and he can't count on a paycheck with his employer behind bars."

"The Deejay?"

"Yeah."

"Is Gareth under arrest?"

"No, but we're watching him."

I forced myself to ask, "What if *he* hired the Shooter?"

"Even if he did, he'd gain nothing by having you killed now."

"I hope you're right."

"If it helps any," he said, "you're still on the list for an hourly drive-by."

"Have to do, I guess." At that point, I was too tired to worry about it.

CHAPTER 25

I slept through the afternoon, got up about six and washed off standing at the sink. Both eyes were black; a butterfly-shaped metal guard was taped over my nose, and I was swaddled from waist to armpits in a sand-colored elastic bandage that supported my damaged ribs. I looked like The Mummy and felt older than Anna Mae.

I put on pajamas, which I never wear, a robe, and slippers, then went downstairs to heat some soup and grill a cheese sandwich. After supper, I went into the study to read.

When the doorbell rang, I jumped a foot in the air. I snatched up the heavy metal hole-punch from my desk and carried it with me down the hall. But instead of a Cuban hitman, I found my favorite Irish-American detective standing on the doorstep.

She swept in bearing two bottles of champagne and informed me in no uncertain terms that we were going to celebrate. I didn't bother to ask what we were celebrating, being in no condition to argue.

By the time we cracked the second bottle, Molly had developed a rosy glow in her cheeks and an added sparkle in her eyes.

"I talked to my uncle about you," she said.

"Who's your uncle?"

"Buddy Malcowitz, the scout for the Sox?"

"Buddy's your uncle? I know Buddy."

"He remembers you, too."

"Haven't seen him in years."

"Said he always had big hopes for you."

"Didn't we all?"

"Said he had them right up until the Sanchez incident."

"Incident? Is that what Buddy called it?"

"Well, no." She grinned fondly. "He said something about your sending Sanchez to 'that happy hacienda in the sky.'"

I laughed. "That sounds more like Buddy."

"He said what happened to you could have happened to anybody, and it was a wonder more pitchers didn't kill people."

"Just me and Carl May."

"He said May had it easier because it happened in nineteen twenty, and he didn't have to watch himself kill Ray Chapman on the evening news along with another fifty million Americans. Buddy told me he walked into the clubhouse that night and saw you watching replays. Said he knew right then you'd never pitch again."

I remembered those replays. "I went over to ask Cappy Parkes to turn off the TV, but I couldn't tear my eyes away from the screen. It didn't look real. I'd seen hundreds of stuntmen die more convincingly. There was no drama in it. Just plop, and down he went."

Molly waited.

"I hated him."

"Why?"

"Because he hated *me*."

"Why?"

"It's complicated."

"Jealousy?"

"That was part of it."

"His or yours?"

148

"Both. We were prospects, stars in amateur ball, me in college, Domingo in Puerto Rico. For the first time in our lives we had to share the spotlight, and we didn't always handle it too well. Our first fight came on the night he booted a double-play ball that would have given me a shutout but ended up costing me the game. I made some comment as I passed his locker, and he gave me a shove. He suggested we meet in the parking lot, and I made the mistake of taking him up on it. I was never much of a fighter, and Domingo was the Puerto Rican middleweight champ in his teens, so it wasn't pretty. While I loped after him trying to guard various portions of my anatomy, he danced around connecting whenever he took a notion. I never landed a punch, but I managed to break a finger on my pitching hand on the side of a Toyota." Molly smiled. "Sounds funny now. But it seemed like the end of the world at the time."

"What happened?"

"Domingo was given a suspension, and I sat out the last six weeks of the season." I took a sip of warm, fizzless champagne. "He got married during the winter to a Puerto Rican girl, who was eighteen and couldn't stand to wear clothes. She'd show up at practice in mostly skin and caused such havoc in fielding drills that she was finally barred. But that didn't stop the rumors, and they eventually got around to me.

"Domingo came at me with a bat the first time, and it took half the team to pull him off. A few days later, he sucker-punched me as I stepped into the shower, then stood there waiting for me to move. This time, I had the sense to stay put, and the management made him stop it for a while after that. But a few weeks later he started writing me notes. He'd leave them in my glove or stuff them into my shoes, notes offering to meet me at various places to settle things once and for all.

"I turned down so many of these invitations that he finally took the direct approach. I came back to my room one night and found him waiting for me with a knife. This time, *I* had the bat and managed to hold him off long enough for help to arrive in the form of Juice and Pappy Parkes. And Domingo was traded two days later."

My throat was dry from talking, and I took another swallow

of wine. "I remember the night it happened like I remember Juice's death. It was a sticky evening with maybe a thousand people in the stands. There were flies and mosquitoes buzzing the mound, and I hated that. I was three runs up with a shutout going in the seventh when Domingo tomahawked a two-run homer and taunted me on his way around the bases. It wasn't the first time he'd showboated at my expense, but I'd just been sent down, and I was in no mood for it.

"I got out of the inning with no more damage and gave up only two harmless singles in the eighth. But after a groundout and strikeout in the ninth, a bloop single put the tying run on first. Domingo was up next, and he'd been hitting me hard all night, so Juice jogged out to see if I wanted to walk him. I told him no, saying I didn't want to walk a runner into scoring position. But what I really wanted was to strike Domingo out.

"I got ahead of him with a fastball that nicked the outside corner for a called strike. Then he waved at an outside curve. After wasting a pitch in the dirt, I went for the third strike on an outside fastball. But he got the head of the bat on it and sent it four hundred feet to right, hooking just foul at the last second. When he got back in the box, he pointed the bat at me and held it there until I started my windup. This time, I tried to bust him in on the hands, but he stepped back and got the sweet part of the bat on it again and drilled it another four hundred feet down the left-field line—foul by inches.

"I figured he expected me to go outside again with a curve ball, so I shook off the curve and nodded at a tight hard one. Domingo once more pointed his bat at me and grinned as I went into my windup. He strode into the plate going for that outside curve, just as I knew he would, and by the time he realized it was coming in it was too late. He spun away, directly into the path of the ball, inadvertently knocking his batting helmet out of position. The ball caught him just behind the left ear"—I touched the spot on my head—"and he dropped like a sack of potatoes.

"I came off the mound in a kind of daze, amazed the ball had hit him. I had lousy control because my fastball moved so much. It always danced at the end, swerving or swooping, right, left, up-and-in, or down-and-away. But this one had traveled as straight and true as a laser beam.

"I knew he was hurt, knocked out at least, and I didn't feel good about that. But I was still in the game, still thinking about getting the last out, half my mind already moving on to the next batter. Juice was kneeling beside Domingo, talking to him, and the ump was looking officious, making sure nobody took the opportunity to start any trouble.

"The trainer came running out of the visitor's dugout to take over from Juice. The crowd was hushed, and I heard the trainer tell Domingo, 'Just lay there.' He touched him on the back and said something else I didn't catch, then reached for Domingo's wrist. When he started feeling for the artery in the neck I knew the situation was more serious than I'd thought. When he told his manager, 'I can't find a pulse,' everything went hazy. I don't know how I got back to the clubhouse. The next thing I remember is walking over to ask Cappy to turn off the television."

Molly shifted uncomfortably, looked away, then back. "You didn't *mean* to kill him."

"Didn't I?"

A beat, then quietly, "Did you?"

"I've asked myself that a thousand times. Everybody knows you have to pitch inside to win, but there's a mighty thin line between throwing inside and throwing *at* somebody. And after all these years, I'm still not sure on which side of the line I stood when I made that pitch."

I lifted my glass but found it empty. "They told me he felt nothing, that his death was instantaneous. But I never could get a grip on that word. Instantaneous. What does it mean exactly? How long does it last? That's the question, isn't it? And I never could get anybody to give me a good answer."

We sat in silence for a while after that, several minutes at least. Then Molly nodded to herself, got up and poured the last of the champagne into my glass. Standing close enough for me to smell her Chanel No.5, she said quietly, "I'm too drunk to drive."

"Would you like to stay?"

151

"Would you like me to?"

Once upstairs, she helped me out of my robe, then guided me to the bed and lay down beside me, fully clothed. She caressed my bandaged shoulder, ribs, and face with her gentle hands, applying cool lips to what bare flesh she could find. Then she stood and undressed for me. She wasn't wearing much—blouse and skirt, bra and panties—but she made them last. I was delighted to discover she had freckles all over, and I wanted to kiss each one. But Molly insisted that I was an injured man and should save my energy. I asked, "For what?" and she showed me. She was right. Neither of us suffered from the experience, but it was no exercise for the frail of limb or faint of heart.

CHAPTER 26

awoke with a headache, then saw Molly wriggling into her panties and forgot all about my head. "Whatimeizit?"

"About seven."

When she came over to give me a kiss, I pulled her down beside me. "You gotta go?"

"Uh-huh."

"Now?"

"Yep."

"You sure?"

She wasn't, and both of us were late for work.

I didn't do much that morning except get in the way, but I stuck it out.

Molly called at lunch time. "Hi," she said, "this is Molly."

"I know."

"Well"—she laughed nervously—"of course you do."

"How are you?"

"Me? I'm okay . . . pretty good, in fact."

"Me, too."

We were silent for a moment, then tried to speak at the same time.

"Go ahead," she said.

"No, you."

We shared a laugh at how clumsy we were being, then she whispered, "I've been thinking about last night."

"You, too?"

"What're we gonna do about it?"

"How about having dinner with me?"

"I have to drive up to Houston, but I should be back by eight."

"Then we'll make it a late supper, someplace fancy. How about the Wentil Trap? Say about ten?"

"Sounds perfect."

I heard another voice. Molly said something away from the phone, then told me, "I gotta go now. But I'll see you tonight."

"I can't wait."

"Me neither." She giggled.

We were acting pretty silly, but we couldn't help it.

That afternoon, Leggy and Randy went off to help with a move-out, Tony handled the office, and I puttered around at the back of the warehouse trying to repair a storage box that was coming apart. We had a big storage load due in at three, but it didn't show up until six, and they didn't finish unloading it until around seven-thirty. Then I sent the others home and told Tony I'd lock up.

"Sure you feel up to it?"

"Worried about me?"

"I've seen you look better."

"God, I hope so."

After they left, I sat on the dock and soaked up the evening, thinking of Molly. Our date wasn't until ten, so I was in no rush to get home.

A few minutes after eight, I strolled down the first row of storage boxes and headed across the back of the warehouse to check the fire exits. The first pair of double doors was closed, chained, and padlocked. This was strictly against the fire code, of course, but it was a habit we had picked up from the previous owners. The doors at the other end were unchained and wedged open a crack. Leggy did that sometimes when he stepped out to suck a joint.

I pulled out the wedge and was attaching the chain when the phone buzzed up front. As I started across the temporary storage area, I heard the unmistakable hum-and-rattle of one of the big power doors closing.

I called, "Tony?"

No answer.

"Leggy?"

I wove my way through plastic-covered couches and chairs, around bed frames and chests of drawers. And the phone stopped buzzing.

"Randy?"

Then I stepped around a tall shipping crate and froze. A man stood about ten feet away: six-five, 260, midnight black, shoulders hunched with muscle, eyes the yellow of old newspapers. He wore jeans and a pullover this time, instead of black sweats, but I knew him.

He didn't say anything. And he didn't move. Until I did.

When I took a step back, he vanished. No magic. He just stepped to the right behind a packing crate. Out of sight but not out of mind.

Where's the Shooter?

I moved between a stack of boxed lawn mowers and a shipment of acoustical tile, then heard a sound behind me.

It was the Linebacker again. He was following now, in no hurry but coming on. My only thought was to stay out of reach, so I cut to the right. I moved past boxes of garden furniture, bicycles, and assorted sporting goods, then stopped again.

The Linebacker was leaning on the back of a couch at the end of the aisle.

"You don't want me to go this way? Is that it?"

He didn't say, just leaned there with his arms crossed.

I backed away keeping an eye on him, then had the itchy feeling of being watched and glanced over my shoulder. There was nobody there, but the Linebacker was gone when I looked back.

I worked my way cautiously to the front of the warehouse, then paused and looked both ways before heading for the controls of the nearest power door.

As I started across, I heard steps to my left and saw the Linebacker moving to cut me off. When I stopped, he stopped. When I started backing in the general direction of the office, he followed at my pace.

I turned as the Shooter glided out from between the last two rows of storage boxes. It was the same elegant figure I'd seen outside Jojo's and in the FBI's grainy photos. Molded in bronze and black, bronze flesh with a polished sheen, black hair in a fashionable cut, white teeth gleaming. He held the automatic at his side, hardly noticeable unless you knew to look for it. I knew.

"Who are you?" I demanded.

"You don't know?"

"I know you kill people."

He shook his head. "I am disappointed."

"Who *are* you?"

"I wrote you a letter."

"When?"

"Ten years ago."

"I don't—"

"After you killed my brother."

Oh, my God!

He smiled and bowed graciously. "I am Jose Esteban Sanchez."

CHAPTER 27

Y ou must know why I am here."

"I never wanted to kill your brother."

The smile didn't waver. "That is a lie."

"We weren't friends, but—"

"You hated him." He sounded disappointed that I would deny it.

"Even if I did, that doesn't mean I wanted to *kill* him."

He tilted his head skeptically. "Really?"

"Really." Honestly? Truly? "He hated *me*."

"Because you disgraced him with his wife."

"I *didn't*. I never touched her. Not once. Ever. I tried to tell him that, but he wouldn't listen. He was crazy on the subject."

"She slept with other ballplayers."

"Maybe so. But not with *me*."

He examined me, still smiling, then nodded. "She may have lied. It is possible. My brother might have been mistaken. But"—he shrugged—"you killed him."

"I didn't *mean* to. I was only trying to move him off the plate."

He shook his head, a slow tick-tock. "I saw you on television. I looked into your eyes as you threw the ball."

"No."

"Yes." The disappointment was back.

"I was coming inside. Every pitcher does it, but nobody dies from it."

"Except—"

"Except this time. I *know*. That's why I quit."

He wasn't buying it. "You wanted to kill him."

"If you were so hot to avenge your brother's death," I snapped, "why'd you wait *ten years*?"

"I was only twelve when it happened, and I had to learn to kill."

"You go to school for that?"

He took it seriously. "I received training, yes, but I also needed experience."

If he wanted to talk, that was okay with me. "How many have you killed?"

"Six, not counting incidental deaths."

"For whom?" I asked, looking around for a weapon. There was a fire extinguisher outside the office and a fireman's axe behind glass, but neither offered much defense against a gun.

"For various governments," he said. "This time for myself."

"I thought it was for your brother." The smile dimmed. "Why'd you kill Juice?"

"He was one of those incidental deaths I mentioned."

"You mean you didn't *plan* to kill him?"

"I didn't even know his name until I saw it in the newspapers."

"Then *why*?"

"Call it an inspired improvisation. I was planning to have my compadre"—he nodded at his oversized friend—"give you a beating. But killing this man who so obviously cared for you seemed like a better way to demonstrate my power. Besides, he tried to interfere."

"He thought you were somebody else."

"I know that now."

158

"Why didn't you kill *me* when you had the chance?"

To him, it was obvious. "You weren't properly prepared."

"For what?"

"You weren't frightened enough."

"That's what you're waiting for now?"

"Exactly." The grin widened. "But I also had another reason to delay."

"Which was?"

"Don't you know what today is?"

"Tuesday."

"And?"

"August third."

"And?"

"What?"

"The tenth anniversary of my brother's death."

He grinned broadly, and I knew I couldn't afford to stand there any longer. I started past him, then froze as he raised his weapon.

He said, "I can take you apart with this." The silencer went *foot!*, and I felt the slug gust past my nose. I stepped back, and a second slug ruffled the hair at the back of my head.

This prompted a raspy laugh from the Linebacker, and the Shooter turned to him with a grin.

As he turned, I moved, heading for the office. The door was open, only a few strides away. The muscles in my back tightened in anticipation of the Shooter's bullet, but I kept moving. I could get out through the office. I'd left the key in the lock. Three strides. Two.

I leapt through the opening and lunged for the outside door. But the knob wouldn't turn. The door was locked. The key was gone. And it wouldn't open without a key.

There was a crowbar in the tool chest under the counter. It would give me a weapon at least. But, when I made it around the counter, I saw no tool chest—no crowbar—and remembered I'd left the tools at the back of the warehouse, where I'd been working on the storage box.

I had to find something. Couldn't just let the Shooter kill me. Had to put up a fight. But with *what*? I stepped around the desk,

159

kicked my chair out of the way, and snatched up the metal in-and-out trays, thinking they'd give me something to throw. Then I saw something else, something rolling across the top of the desk, and threw down the trays, letting the object drop into my hand: the brass baseball. Juice's gift.

The Shooter glided through the warehouse door smiling as I grasped the ball across the seams. I toed the rubber, rocked and coiled, bringing my arm back as he turned. As his hand came up, I drove forward, bringing my arm over, and released the ball straight at his face. Before it hit, his slug kicked me in the left shoulder and spun me around.

I turned back as the Shooter slammed into the outside door. He hung there for a moment, face frozen in an expression of surprise. Then his eyes rolled up into their sockets; the gun slipped from his fingers, and he followed it limply to the floor.

CHAPTER 28

The Linebacker charged through the door to the warehouse and ducked down to examine his partner. When he stood, his back was arched like a cat's. He focused on me, eyes widening as he moved around the counter. If he had a gun, he didn't bother to pull it. He intended to take me apart with his hands.

I scrambled onto the desk and banged my head on the ceiling as I jumped to the counter. The Linebacker snatched at my leg, but I kept moving, dropping from the counter to the floor.

The landing drove a spike into my shoulder, and the room darkened. I might have passed out if the Linebacker's growls hadn't kept me awake. I knew there was a gun on the floor, but I didn't see it, and he didn't give me time to look for it. He was over the counter before I cleared the door.

Each stride drove the spike a little deeper, but I ran on. I punched the red UP button on the first power door, but it rose too slowly for me to get out, and I couldn't stop. I veered left into the short-term storage area, toppled a stack of boxes into his path, and ran on as he went down. Then I cut around a shipping crate, spotted a fire extinguisher attached to a vertical support post, and pulled it down with my good hand.

It was heavier than I expected and slipped from my grip, clanging to the concrete. But I pinned it with a foot, found the handle, and jerked it off the floor as the Linebacker appeared.

I aimed the sudsy stream at his face, but he threw up his hands to block it. Then I turned it on the floor, and his feet slipped out from under him. He landed with a gratifying groan, and I feebly tossed the extinguisher in his direction before taking off.

The fire door was just to my right, but it was chained and padlocked, and the bad guys had the keys. So I veered left and headed across the back of the warehouse, blood running down my left arm, shoulder jolted by every footfall. My plan was to circle around and beat him back to the power door. But as I turned into the aisle between the last two rows of storage boxes, I saw my move had been anticipated.

The Linebacker was leaning casually against a box at the end of the aisle.

I knew I'd made a mistake. Here my options were too limited. There were only two exits from each aisle, and all Mr. Olympus had to do was wait up front until I appeared at one of them.

I retreated slowly to the end of the aisle. Then, thinking he'd expect me to turn left back toward short-term storage, I stepped to the right and out of sight. It had the virtue of being unexpected. But what now?

C'mon, brain! Focus!

The tool box sat in the corner about twenty feet away. It contained some things that might be used as weapons, but I was fading too fast for that. My left side was drenched with blood; the darkness was moving in, and I was in no shape to battle the Linebacker, with or without a weapon.

What I was looking for was a place to hide; what I saw was the ladder. It was attached to a vertical support post leading up to a system of high catwalks. I knew I'd never be able to make it as far as the catwalks, but I thought I should be able to reach the top of the boxes. He might not expect that.

Climbing the ladder proved even harder than expected. My left arm was useless, so I had to climb with one hand. I'd hook my chin over a rung for balance, grab another with my right hand, then pull up while pushing with my legs.

My progress was agonizingly slow, and I kept expecting the Linebacker to appear. But I couldn't spare the energy to look for him. Each rung required more effort, and each new effort was more difficult to produce.

Halfway up, I knew I'd never make it. My heart was slamming into my injured rib; my head was spinning. I couldn't catch a breath, and my legs were trembling like a toddler's. I only kept going because it was too late to do anything else.

Just when I was sure I'd never be able to climb another rung, I realized I didn't have to. I was already there. All I had to do was make the transfer to the top of the boxes.

My goal was about three feet away on the other side of the post. I had to stretch my leg around and lean out to reach it with my foot. I made it that far—one foot resting on the box, one on the ladder—then couldn't go any farther.

I locked my right arm around the ladder and rested my face against the cool steel post for a moment, trying to gather my strength. But what remained was pouring out with my blood and sweat, and just holding on was almost more than I could manage.

So I took a couple of breaths, then worked my right foot to the back of the ladder and shifted my right hand to the box side of the post. But reaching across my chest shoved me away from the post, and I suddenly felt myself falling backward.

Throwing all my strength into my right arm, I pushed off the post. I was toppling in the right direction when my left foot slipped, and I caught the edge of a box across the thighs as my chin hammered into the plywood.

CHAPTER 29

don't know how long I was out, but I was still on top of the boxes, sticking over the edge from the thighs down. I assumed the Linebacker had heard my landing, but I didn't see him.

When I tried to stand, the room started to spin, and I decided to crawl instead. I couldn't even do that in the normal sense with one arm. The best I could manage was to scoot along on my knees using my right hand for balance.

All I wanted to do was lie down for a few hours, but I knew the Linebacker would eventually think to look on top of the boxes, so I kept moving. I didn't see how I'd ever be able to get down the ladder at the other end, but I wasn't going to worry about that till I got there.

I was halfway down the row when I risked a glance over my shoulder and saw the Linebacker stepping onto the top. He grinned.

I picked up speed, whimpering and talking to myself. "Move it, you son-of-a-bitch! Move it!"

He came on slowly, knowing I couldn't escape.

164

"Get up!" I told myself. "Can't die on your knees! Get up!"

I did. The world spun crazily, but I was up. Not for long, however. I waddled forward only a half-dozen steps before the boxes jumped up and smacked me.

The scene browned out, but I didn't let it go black. If I did, I was dead. I was probably dead anyway, but I had to keep moving.

Where was he?

I looked back. He was close, *too* close. Standing just ten feet away, watching me.

"You bastard," I said.

He grinned smugly and came on, catlike.

I started crawling again, moving as fast as I could. But he was closing quickly now. When he stopped one stride back and gave me the Shooter's slow tick-tock shake of the head, I suddenly ran out of gas.

I had exhausted all my resources of anger, and even the pain was at an ebb. My body no longer felt like my own. I sat and watched with simple curiosity as the Linebacker slipped a hand into his back pocket.

He pulled out a slender pearl handle and, with a snap of his wrist, flicked a blade into position.

I hadn't expected a knife. Given the man's bulk and my condition, any weapon but his hands seemed superfluous. But there it was, glinting with light.

He balanced it tip down on his palm, flipped it, caught it by the handle, and carved intricate patterns in the air.

His warmup complete, he held out a muscular forearm for my inspection. It was very dark brown, almost black, rippling with sinew and writhing with arterial snakes. He ran the edge of the blade lightly across the surface, and I was watching tiny dark red beads appear along the line when his hand flicked out.

I jerked back, but the blade touched me on the forehead. It was only a touch, and I wasn't sure he'd cut me until I felt the blood trickling down my face.

He caught me on the chin as I scooted backward, then on my good arm. When I pulled it away, he cut my cheek. When I turned, he got the other cheek.

Then he stopped to clean his weapon, running the blade up and down his leg like a razor on a strop. And I used the break to wipe the blood out of my eyes. At that point, it was the best I could do.

When his blade shone like a mirror, he flourished it across his throat to let me know what he was planning. Then he moved in.

I was scrambling backward when I heard a blast.

The Linebacker retreated a step and slapped the side of his head. He stared at the blood on his hand in confusion, then glared at me and stepped forward again. As his foot landed, two more quick blasts sent him stumbling backward. He tripped, went down hard, and lay still for a moment. Just when I was sure he was down for the count, he rolled over and pushed himself up onto his knees, facing away from me. After pausing to gather his strength, he rocked back and got his feet under him and actually managed to fight his way upright. He stood there swaying drunkenly for a moment before realizing he was facing in the wrong direction. Then he turned, caught his balance, and grinned broadly when he saw me. But, as he lifted his foot, his eyes lost focus, and he paused. He raised his hands to his head, took a breath like he was going to say something, then slowly toppled, like a giant tree, in the other direction. He landed with a crash that sent a tremble through the whole row of boxes, his head cracking into the plywood and bouncing. I thought he was dead until I saw his chest rising. It rose slowly and fell, rose and fell. Then he lifted his head to give me one last yellow-eyed stare and collapsed with a rattling sigh.

When I turned to see Molly and Willis peeking around opposite sides of the post, I figured it was safe to close my eyes.

A few seconds later, I heard, "You all right, Bull?" and looked up to see Molly's anxious face hanging over me.

"That's a silly question," I said.

She smiled. "Sorry."

"You called me Bull."

"Did I?"

"You did."

She crossed her heart. "Won't happen again."

"What're you doing here?"

166

"I got no answer when I called. When I didn't get one at your house either, I sent cars there, then grabbed Jake and beat it over here."

"You're a wonder."

"You're not so bad yourself." She borrowed a handkerchief from Willis and pressed it to my shoulder.

"Guess we'll have to postpone our date for tonight," I said. "Will you wait for me?"

"You're only going to the hospital," she replied, "not prison."

"It's a fast world we live in."

She laughed and called to Willis, "Jake, would you see about getting a stretcher up here?"

He said, "Yay-uh," and started down the ladder.

"Now that he's out of the way," I said, "how about a kiss?"

She grinned. "I guess you deserve one. If I can find a place that isn't bleeding."

"What about my mouth?"

Parkinson dropped by my hospital room the next morning. He walked in and sat down, stretched out his legs and clasped his hands behind his head, looking relaxed for the first time since I'd met him. "No wonder we couldn't crack this one," he said. "It was *two* cases."

"Is the Shooter dead?"

"Oh, yeah. The force of your pitch jabbed a fragment of nasal bone into his brain. And slamming his head into the door must have finished him. Coroner said he was gone before he hit the floor."

"Hope he doesn't have another brother."

"No, Miguel and Graciela Sanchez had only two sons."

"How old is the father?"

He smiled.

Molly came by on her lunch break. "The doctors say you're a lucky man."

"Yeah, but I think they hold it against me."

She grinned. "No challenge."

"Hell of an attitude."

"They're like cops."

"How's that?"

"We'll take a murder over a traffic violation any day. So, how's the shoulder?"

"The slug missed the joint and only chipped the bone."

"Hurt?"

"They've got me so doped up I hardly know I *have* a shoulder."

She eyed the bandages on my face. "How about the cuts?"

"They were disappointed about that, too. None of the major facial muscles were severed, but they tell me I'll have some neat scars."

"Ah," she said. "More character."

"Any more and I'll look like Rocky Graziano."

Molly had just left when Tony stuck his head in the door and asked, "How you doin'?"

"Not as bad as I look. Who's minding the store?"

"I left Leggy in charge. We had something we thought you ought to see. This came in the mail for you today."

It was an envelope in a transparent plastic sleeve, with a white card on the back that was addressed to "Dear Postal Customer." It went on at some length to explain that, against great odds and in spite of the "highly sophisticated mechanical/electrical systems utilized by the Postal Service to ensure our customers prompt delivery of their mail," my letter had been "damaged in handling." Mislaid, too, apparently, since it had taken nearly three weeks to make it across town.

The enclosed envelope had been ripped open, and a stain that looked like grease covered most of the address. But it was the handwriting that caught my eye.

It was Juice's.

CHAPTER 30

Bull,

Well I fucked up just like you always said I would. I can't see no way around it except to get out of town, but I figured I owed you some kind of explanation before I go.

You know about me running errands for Dylan like driving Syb up to Hobby Airport and stuff like that. Well about a year ago he gave me $200 to pick up two suitcases in Texas City. And after that I'd get the call to go after those suitcases about once a month.

The longer it went on the more curious I got, but whenever I'd ask Dylan about it he'd just laugh and say he guessed he'd have to get somebody else to pick up the suitcases. I didn't want him to do that on account of I needed the money, so I'd just go on with it for another month.

Last Saturday he called and asked me to go to the picnic grounds across the Bolivar Ferry Monday at noon. I done everything like he said, but when I tried to

169

deliver the suitcases they wasn't nobody home. Dylan called that night and told me he was stuck down in the islands somewheres and asked me to take care of his suitcases until he got back the next day.

Well they say curiosity killed the cat and I reckon I must have some cat in me because I couldn't get those suitcases out of my head. I couldn't sleep for thinking about them. And you know me old buddy. You always said I'd sleep through the end of the world.

Anyway, I finally couldn't take it no more and cut the seals on one and I never seen so much money all in one place. I counted out close to $100,000 in that first case and I should have known right then I was in trouble. But I was only thinking that $200 wasn't enough commission on $200,000.

Tuesday morning I dropped by the warehouse and put the suitcases in a box. Then I went out to see Dylan. He was awful pissed about me opening them suitcases, but he finally cooled down and we settled on $5,000 as a fair commission.

When I got back to the warehouse I like to have had a heart attack on account of you was working on the boxes and the suitcases wasn't where I had put them and I couldn't find the contract. Since you wouldn't talk to me I figured I'd come back later. But I got hung up in a poker game down at the Seaman's Center and I didn't get away until after the warehouse was locked up. And I was too drunk by then to do anything but head on home.

I went through the files on Wednesday but still couldn't find the contract. You run me out of the office and wouldn't talk to me, so I decided to come back after you shut down. But that afternoon three men come busting into my house and told me I had to come up with the suitcases or the cocaine. I tried to tell them that was the first I'd heard about any cocaine, but they didn't believe me.

The next day I called Dylan to find out what was

going on and he didn't want to talk about it on the phone, so I went out to see him. He finally admitted he didn't have the cocaine because the deal had fallen through and I told him there were some guys out to beat my ass. He said it was his fault and that I should get out of town until he could get it tooken care of. He give me $5000 dollars and promised to send me another $20,000 when I got to where I was going.

But the first thing I did was to go home to get my scrapbook and wrote this letter because I couldn't just up and leave without explaining why I stole that money from you. I know I shouldn't have done it, but I owed Rufus Jones and he was threatening to have his Indian break both my arms if I didn't pay him.

I know they wasn't no excuse for it, but I hope you can find it in your heart to forgive me.

Your friend,
Juice

There was another page in a different colored ink. It explained that he hadn't made it out of town because the Deejay's boys had been waiting for him outside Conchita's house the next morning. They'd taken his $5000 and had beaten him until he'd told them that there was no cocaine and that he couldn't find the money because I had moved it.

. . . I know I shouldn't have told them that Bull. I never wanted to get you into this, but I couldn't help it.

Anyway, they give me till midnight to come up with the money. If I don't, the boss man told me I'd have to get you to help me find it. I'm real sorry about that old buddy.

Juice

CHAPTER 31

Thursday was my day to receive flowers. They came from the Merchants' Association, from Anna Mae, and from the boys at the warehouse. I even got some roses from Julie Brauer and Jeremy Parker, with an attached card expressing their sincerest wishes for a speedy recovery.

Later that afternoon, Molly came by with an unexpected get-well present from Mariano Santiago—a pencil drawing of me pitching. It caught me striding toward the plate, right leg at full stretch behind me, left foot planted for the drive, arm cocked, eyes on the target and a fierce look of concentration on my face.

"He's good," Molly said.

"Sure is. Did he tell you why he wanted me to have this?"

"No. He just asked me to give it to you."

That was Mariano: enigmatic to the end. Whatever it meant, it was without a doubt the most significant communication we'd ever shared.

I left the hospital Friday morning with my arm in a sling, my shoulder bandaged, my ribs wrapped, and my face stitched like a road-show Frankenstein. I cabbed it to the warehouse and borrowed Tony's Buick automatic because I couldn't handle shifting my pickup's gears with one arm.

Gareth had been arrested after I'd given the police Juice's letter, but he was already out on bail, and he called me shortly after I got home.

"How's the Bull?" he asked with his usual droll heartiness.

"Pretty bearish right now."

He chuckled. "We're grilling steaks. Why don't you drive out and claim one?"

It felt strange talking to him, as though *I* were the one caught in a lie. "Thanks, but I'll probably go to bed early."

He insisted quietly, "There are matters we need to discuss."

"You don't owe me an explanation."

"I think I do," he said. "If you're not up to driving, I could come after you."

Knowing he wasn't going to take no for an answer, I said, "I can manage. Seven o'clock?"

"See you then."

We were stiff with each other at first, not knowing quite what to say. The steaks and a few Foster's loosened our tongues, but there was still a distance that had never been there before.

After dinner, we retired to the living room couch. We were swapping tales of Juice's exploits when Gareth suddenly turned serious on me. "I'm glad you know I had nothing to do with killing him. I couldn't have stood that."

I said half jokingly, "You'll stand worse."

He winced, glancing away. "No more than I deserve, you mean?"

"I didn't say that."

"I may have used Juice," he said, "but my friendship was genuine."

I lifted my good shoulder in a semishrug. "What good are friends if you can't use them?"

"Christ, that's cynical," he said with a laugh.

"Did the police tell you about his letter?"

"They said it implicated me."

"I gave it to them."

Beat. "Did you?"

I nodded.

"No need to apologize," he said.

"I wasn't apologizing. I just thought you should know."

He stared at me for a moment, then laid a hand on my shoulder. "You did what you had to do. I understand that."

"Do you really?"

"You don't believe me?"

"I don't know what to believe."

He took his hand away. "What's got you puzzled?"

"This whole thing. I've always loved mysteries, but this may put me off them for good. I had Julie Brauer picked out as the culprit. That would have been perfect. I never liked him. But—"

"Not me."

"No."

He sighed. "No."

I sipped my beer, examining Sybil, who sat across from us. She looked ten years older than the last time I'd seen her.

Turning to Gareth, I said, "Can I ask you something?"

He sighed again. "Why I did it?"

I nodded.

He sat up straight, squaring his shoulders. "I haven't admitted doing anything, you know."

"They have a pretty good case."

"Oh"—he shrugged it off—"I'm not saying they won't convict me, but I don't intend to make it easy for them. However," he added with a grin, "on a purely hypothetical level, if I *were* to have committed the alleged crime, it would have been for the money. A five hundred percent return could certainly be tempting." He chuckled to himself.

"What's the joke?"

"Still speaking hypothetically, if I were to have done such a thing, I'd have to say that Juice had given me the idea."

"How?"

"He brought some cocaine out here one evening—after New Years, I think it was, in 'eighty. Easy money, he said, and fed me the whole story—where he bought it, how much he paid for it, how it was smuggled in, and how much he made on the deal."

"So you decided to try it yourself?"

"Maybe not immediately. But if, at a later date in—'eighty-two, for example, when the Bust turned my oil stock into so much low-grade toilet paper—I might have recalled the conversation."

"That's all it was?" I asked. "A way to cover your investment losses?"

"It might have started out that way, but . . ." He trailed off with a shrug.

"Easy money's hard to resist?"

"Difficult, to say the least."

"And what were you planning to do with all this hypothetical cash?"

He snuggled down, resting his chin on his beer can. "If I were smart, I'd've already done it. Bought myself an island, or something equally sensible."

"An island? Where?"

He laid a long finger to the side of his nose. "It wouldn't be very wise for this hypothetical criminal to reveal details to somebody who's likely to be called as a prosecution witness, now would it? If I had acquired such ill-gotten gain, I'd undoubtedly wish to keep some of it."

"Undoubtedly."

He made like the Cheshire cat as he sprawled back on the couch, but his grin soon wilted. "You know what I feel guiltiest about?"

"What?"

"Two things." He looked at Sybil. "One, was getting *you* into this."

175

She stood and came over to sit beside him. "I should have stopped you."

"You tried."

"Not hard enough."

He turned back to me. "My other regret is that Juice had to face Wheeler alone. I gave him the money to leave, but he didn't go. I should have seen that he did."

"You didn't kill him."

"He wouldn't have been there that night if not for me."

"And he wouldn't have been shot if I hadn't killed Domingo Sanchez."

He shook his head, then rested it on the back of the couch and stared at the ceiling. He said sadly, "A natural victim, our Juice."

"Putty in the hand," I agreed.

When I got up to leave, Syb gave me a hug, and Gareth walked me out to the car.

"Maybe some day you'll come visit my hypothetical island," he said.

We shared a grin, but the best I could offer was "Maybe."

I didn't know quite how to feel about Gareth. I suppose most people would have found it simple enough—he's a drug dealer; lynch him! But, being one of those tens of millions of Americans who *use* illegal drugs, I couldn't get very self-righteous about those who *sell* them. I didn't put pot and coke in the same category, of course, but the law did.

I know everybody is supposed to want a drug-free America these days. But the phrase "drug-free" was never intended to be taken literally. What it really meant was that those who had claimed their drugs first, drugs like tobacco or alcohol, got to keep them, while the rest of us had to choose from their list or do without.

I suspect it was heartening for the vice-ridden everywhere to hear a number of politicians, including a recent law-and-order nominee to the U.S. Supreme Court, confess to having used controlled substances. Naturally, all of them claim to have since turned away from these insidious paths, but you can't always believe everything politicians say.

Prohibition doesn't work. It was tried before, with the same results: lots of money was spent; lots of people died; and the prohibited substances kept pouring in. Why? It's simple. The harder you try to enforce an unenforceable law the richer you make those who break it.

I believe in the rule of law, but proponents of its strictest application are often quick enough to ignore or pervert certain statutes when it serves their purposes. Ask Dick Nixon or Ronnie Reagan. And, as far as I'm concerned, Gareth's crime was at least one level below trashing the Constitution or selling weapons to terrorists. One might argue that it isn't a matter of crime but of motive, but I've also never been convinced that the service of personal power or national pride is any more defensible as an excuse for wrongdoing than greed.

On the other hand, as Anna Mae had put it, "Folks are gettin' shot over that cocaine." Gareth had put Juice in danger and had done too little too late to protect him. And if he managed to avoid being involved in killing, it was only a matter of luck. His greed had made him reckless enough to think he could get away with it, and he'd earned a prison sentence for his recklessness.

But he was still my friend. That hadn't changed. If I was called upon to testify against him, I'd have to tell what I knew. But that didn't mean I had to turn my back on him. That was one mistake I didn't intend to repeat.

CHAPTER 32

I dropped by Anna Mae's house the next afternoon to tell her about Jose Esteban Sanchez.

"So Harvey was killed for nothing?" she said.

"He was in the wrong place at the wrong time."

She shook her head. "That boy never had a stitch of luck."

She retreated to the kitchen to shed her tears in private, then came back with a pitcher of lemonade and a plate of homemade sweet rolls. "How would you like a beach house?"

"Pardon?"

"I always meant Harvey to have it, but he ain't around no more."

I didn't know what to say. "I'm honored," I told her, "but you must have relatives somewhere with a better claim than me."

"Maybe so, but they all went north or west, and none of 'em ever cared much for Galveston." She rested a withered hand on my shoulder. "So I'd like you to have it." When I tried to respond, she patted me and said, "You think about it. It'll probably cost more than it's worth to fix up, but I'd like to see somebody get a little use out of it." She added with a grin, "All I ask is that you come see me ever now and then."

I stood and gave her a hug. "I think I can manage that."

Molly appeared a few hours after dark and spread out her blanket on the sand without saying anything. I didn't ask how she knew where to find me. By that time, I had come to accept that she could read minds.

It was a cloudless evening. A fat round moon was rising, its reflection fragmenting in the surf. Splendid. Peaceful. Just as Juice had liked it.

"I miss him."

"I know."

The gulf breeze stiffened, kicking up whitecaps beyond the breakers.

"I've been doing some thinking," I said.

"Come to any conclusions?"

"I've decided I have to do something about my life."

That provoked a low whistle.

"You said it. Turns out I have a tendency to follow the path of least resistance."

"You don't say."

"I just did." I picked up a strand of beached kelp. "Like this stuff, I just drift with the tide."

"Sounds pleasant enough."

"For a while."

"Does that mean you're giving up the moving business?"

"I'm thinking of asking Tony if he'd like to take over and maybe use his uncle's inheritance to buy Juice's half."

"What'll *you* do?"

"I haven't gotten that far yet."

"You could finish your book?"

"I don't think so."

"Why not?"

"I may start another one."

"Ah."

"I was also thinking of giving Conchita a piece of the warehouse. I know she could use the money, and she's not likely to get anything from Juice's estate."

Molly punched me lightly on the shoulder. "What a softie."

"And I decided something else."

"What's that?"

"That I have to be more patient with my friends."

"Don't we all?"

"Too late for Juice."

Moonlight flickered in her eyes. "Maybe you'll get another chance."

"With you?"

"I'm here."

"That's true."

"Come to any other life-altering conclusions?"

"Not yet."

"Still working on it?"

"Resting now."

Waves lapped and sighed.

"Want to share my blanket?" she asked.